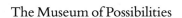

The Museum of Possibilities

THE MUSEUM OF POSSIBILITIES

BARBARA SIBBALD

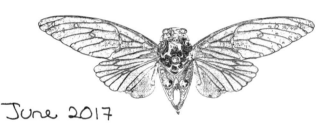

June 2017
  To Elizabeth,
   a Banff buddy + lovely writer.
 A hope you enjoy the possibilities!
       xx Barbara

The Porcupine's Quill

Library and Archives Canada Cataloguing in Publication

Sibbald, Barbara, 1958–, author
    The museum of possibilities / Barbara Sibbald.

Short stories.
ISBN 978-0-88984-400-1 (softcover)

    I. Title.

PS8637.I23M87 2017   C 813'.6   C 2017-900974-5

1   2   3   •   19   18   17

Published by The Porcupine's Quill, 68 Main Street, PO Box 160,
Erin, Ontario N0B 1T0. http://porcupinesquill.ca

Readied for the press by Stephanie Small.

Represented in Canada by Canadian Manda.
Trade orders are available from University of Toronto Press.

We acknowledge the support of the Ontario Arts Council and the Canada
Council for the Arts for our publishing program. The financial support of the
Government of Canada through the Canada Book Fund is also gratefully
acknowledged.

Canada Council   Conseil des arts
for the Arts   du Canada

ONTARIO ARTS COUNCIL
CONSEIL DES ARTS DE L'ONTARIO
an Ontario government agency
un organisme du gouvernement de l'Ontario

Canadä

Ontario
Ontario Media Development
Corporation

For Stuart Kinmond

Contents

PART ONE

The Museum of Possibilities

THE MUSEUM
OF POSSIBILITIES

It's a bloody mess and now he has to take care of it. Three so-called experts, all of them useless. The training isn't what it used to be, he tells anyone who will listen. But no one will. Not anymore. I've passed my best-before, he thinks.

'See what you can do,' his supervisor says, passing him the case file. 'Last chance.' Last chance before Clean Sweep, that is. It's a grand euphemism, the name stolen ages ago from an allegedly reality-TV show with perennially contrived happy endings: rooms piled with junk transformed into orderly, usable space. In his department's real-life incarnation, a crew loads multiple Dumpsters with the client's junk and hauls it away to the recycling centre—another euphemism. If people only knew, he thinks. Everyone conscientiously separates paper, metal, plastic, thinking they're doing their bit for the environment. Meanwhile the collectors dump it all together into a biomass generator. He's seen it himself. The toxic fumes from melted plastic and god knows what else are pumped up north. You think that's a pipeline for gas? Ha! And his clients, post–Clean Sweep? They go to the so-called Restore Spa, to be prodded, poked and then forgotten in some windowless pod, left to their 'later-life narrative'. Some spa—it's a human trash heap, with no attempt made to restore. I'd sooner kill myself than end up there, he thinks.

It's grey. November grey and lightly raining. More of a mist, but with the prophesy of a downpour hanging in the low, dark clouds. He hopes the client, Mrs Petali, is at home. More often than not these stubborn clients will skip out on an appointment. Todd parks his aging car in the crumbling concrete parkade and walks briskly—or at least as briskly as possible given the pain in his ankle. He broke it two years ago, tumbled down a client's cluttered basement steps. Lots of physio. Paid for and now healed, according to them, to Occu-health. He walks through a dead sea of leaves on the sidewalk, ignoring the persistent pain and mentally reviewing the details of the case.

Maria Petali. Her geared-to-income apartment is due for painting. Overdue, in fact. That is the ostensible excuse. No one really cares if these places are painted or maintained. The real reason is the complaints from neighbours of odours, of boxes spilling out into the apartment building's hallways. Those symptoms have been cleared up now, but his department was alerted to the underlying problem: hoarder, grade three. With grade ones you're basically bringing a shovel; there's no use in attempting reason. Grade three is no picnic either. If it is grade three. He's used to these dire prognostications delivered by know-nothing young social workers—those without adequate time in the field, those who are still working from textbook definitions. Still, he is prepared for the worst. One never knows.

Others have failed to resolve Mrs Petali's case, but Todd resolves to be successful in what may be his last challenging case before retirement. He'll show them: his ways, the old ways, they work.

———————

It's an older apartment building, once an architectural showpiece with great, swooping white arches out front, structurally useless but no doubt considered quite avant-garde at the time. The paint is now peeling from the arches, exposing pitted concrete beneath. They'll have to remove those arches in a few years, he thinks as he steps through the front doors. The buzzers don't work—probably haven't for decades—and a grubby sign encrusted with layers of tape proclaims that the elevators are, predictably, out of service. Lucky for him, Mrs Petali is in 312. Third floor—an easy climb for him, but not so easy for the Clean Sweep crew. He makes a note to talk to the super, see if they can get the elevators moving at least for an afternoon. They've probably been shut off to save money, he thinks, the inconvenience promoted as a public health measure to encourage residents to get a bit of exercise.

The third-floor hallway is dimly lit, but surprisingly clean. He expected worse, has seen much worse. He taps forcefully on the door, three raps, so she knows he means business.

'Mrs Petali?' he calls. 'Ma'am?'

He knows from years in the field that it pays to be respectful, to start out on a formal footing. His younger colleagues—and aren't they all younger these days?—guffaw at this notion behind his back. They have quotas to fill, no time for social niceties. He refuses to comply with quotas and has, so far, gotten away with it, probably because he's so close to leaving that no one can be bothered trying to convince him to change. But when push comes to shove, who do they call? Me, he thinks. That's who.

The door opens a crack, a taut chain holding it firmly in place. He can't see inside. 'What do you want?' demands a husky female voice.

'It's Mr Grimshaw. Todd Grimshaw from the SS, Social Services. I'm just here for a chat, Mrs Petali. No cause for alarm.'

'In my dreams,' he hears her mutter as she closes the door. The chain jiggles, the door opens. 'Mr Grimshaw,' she says. 'I've been expecting you.'

He's slightly taken aback; he's not used to a civil welcome. To any welcome at all, come to that. But then she doesn't look like the typical sweatpants-and-stained-T-shirt client. She wears what appear to be layers of skirts—petticoats? he wonders—in dark tones: deep green, perhaps purple. A long-sleeved, shapeless black sweater, unravelling at the hem, covers her upper body. Her hair is bound in an imprecise bun. No makeup. It would be hard to guess her age, but he has the dossier and knows: she's fifty-three.

She turns, walks unevenly down the hall. Is that a limp? He feels a wave of empathy. But she's quick on her feet, turns sideways, shuffles between the stacks of detritus lining both walls and disappears. He closes the door and in his mind he automatically, expertly, begins grouping the junk, like with like. Books, a surprising number and all hardcover, including some large volumes—art books judging by the size of them. He's curious to know which ones she has and whether any go beyond his own extensive collection. Mostly the stacks consist of boxes covered with garish advertising pitching their contents: toasters, blenders, mixers, hair dryers, dishes. He knows from experience that the boxes may or may not contain said items.

'Mrs Petali?' he calls.

There is no response. He sidles down the hall in her wake, turns into a large room. It's quite remarkably proportioned for a building of this vintage, he thinks. The living room, dining room and kitchen are all in one. 'Open concept' it used to be called when such things were popular, before people figured out that these designs couldn't accommodate as much junk. And when the space inevitably filled, the possession-obsessed rented lockers by the millions, because who knew when you might need that ancient Blu-ray DVD player or an extra hand-vacuum? No sense tossing it out. That's where it begins, he thinks with a sigh.

He's proud to live in a seven-hundred-square-foot apartment. Of course, if there had been children … but there weren't and though Gabby, his now ex-wife, had wanted a larger space, his tireless enthusiasm for the minimalist life dominated. Maybe if I'd been more flexible, he thinks, but as usual he dispels the idea. He has to set an example, especially in his line of work.

She, Mrs Petali, stands in a narrow space by the island that divides the kitchentte from the dining and living areas. The latter two are stacked to the ceiling with towers of boxes and books. Just like the hallway, only without passageways. It's a seemingly impenetrable wall.

Mrs Petali is looking through a bag. Now that's a familiar sight, he thinks. These people are always poking through their plastic shopping bags, wanting to show off their latest acquisitions. She pulls out some white fabric, shakes it out. It's a christening gown.

'Beautiful, isn't it?' she says, fingering the pink ribbon that is threaded through the eyelet. 'It's quite old.'

'The fabric is very fine,' he says. 'Is it for your granddaughter? Your niece?'

She frowns and stuffs it back into its white cocoon. Of course, she has neither, he thinks. Showing something beautiful is a common enough ruse to distract him from the bigger problem. Two can play, he thinks.

'Could I bother you for a cup of tea?' he asks. 'It was quite a walk from the parkade.'

He doesn't want the tea. This is his standard discourse, a way of establishing himself as a visitor—again being respectful—and at the same time impressing upon her that she can't even do something as routine as serving a cup of tea to a visitor.

He stares expectantly into the kitchenette. There are mounds of dishes, hummocks of pots. Some are encrusted with black, but not mould—at least not yet. And oddly, there's no smell. Well, perhaps something chemical, but not organic. She likely sprays them with something, he thinks, to mask the odour. There are many such products on the market now. He can see where his colleagues have coerced her into creating some order: empty spaces on the counter, holes in the rubble. He reads the signs his hapless predecessors have left behind.

'Can I help you find the tea?' he asks kindly. It's not a show. He does feel kindly. He wants to help her see her problem, help her to a more normal life.

'No, no!' she says, alarmed.

Then she is silent.

'Okay, Mrs Petali, it's okay.'

He'd like to sit, to rest his aching ankle, but there is no place. All four chairs are stacked high with books and boxes. Even if Mrs Petali wanted to clear one, there's no place to put the stuff. What he can see of the floor is filthy, the patterned linoleum barely discernible. He decides to dive in.

'You know the painters are coming in a week,' he says.

'Yes. The others have been through all that. I don't see why ...'

'You know why,' he says firmly.

'Yes, I suppose I do.'

Progress! he thinks.

'We need to clear the way for them,' he continues. 'So they can do their work. They'll paint one room at a time. Your things will be stacked in the centre and covered with a tarp.'

Her eyes widen; obviously this is news to her.

'I don't have to clear the whole room?'

'Not entirely. But you know there's too much in here now. You have some choices to make. Now, we have a very sweet and efficient young woman ...'

'No!' She shakes her head vigorously. 'No more people. I've had three trooping through here already, telling me what to do. Now you. You're the fourth. That's enough.'

She's right, he thinks. That's way too many. One person should have been able to handle it. Incompetents.

'Okay.' He sighs. 'No others. But that means I'm your last chance before Clean Sweep. You know what that is?'

She nods slowly, looks to him, meeting his eyes for the first time.

'I'm not one of them,' she says.

'One of whom?' he asks.

'You know. Those other people, your colleagues, they never actually said the word. I could see they were afraid of how I would react. I'm not afraid. Hoarder.'

She spits the word out like a hunk of gristle.

'I'm not a hoarder.'

Typical denial, he thinks.

'You think I meet the criteria in the DSM—the Diagnostic and Statistical Manual of Mental Disorders. Grade three, probably,' she continues. 'But that's not it at all. You don't understand.'

'Tell me,' he says. 'But, please, may I sit down? My ankle—I broke it a few years ago....'

'Of course, I should have offered.' She gracefully removes a stack of boxes from one of the chairs, perches them on top of another pile—precariously, it seems to him, yet they stay put.

He sits. His legs are cramped, held in at an odd angle against the press of boxes and books, but his ankle is definitely more at ease. 'Thank you,' he says. 'Now, tell me: What's all this about?'

'You're the first who's asked,' she says. 'I don't like to show unless there's interest. I believe that curiosity is life's force.'

She turns and begins shifting boxes from another pile, finally unearthing the one she wants. Its glossy packaging promises a tool for effortlessly dicing rock-hard root vegetables and pungent onions. She places the box on top of a stack of large books beside him so it's level with his head. Rather than opening the box from the top, she pulls at the sides; it falls open. His mouth falls open. He feels as though he's entered another world.

He's in a tree amidst branches, mottled leaves and roughly textured bark. And there, partly hidden, a nest containing three robin's eggs, the pure blue of a perfect summer sky. A small human finger, a child's, gently touches the edge of the nest. Beyond the nest, other trees tower; it's a forest, yet more. An orchestrated forest. What an ideal forest might look like. A pair of squirrels is poised on a nearby branch; their chatter is almost audible. And he glimpses a deer lying in the grass below, asleep or at rest. Perhaps dead. It's like a set in a play, he thinks. Only real. Yet not.

'It's beautiful,' he says after a moment, aware of the woeful inadequacy of his words. He cannot say more, fears he may begin to cry, though he's not sure why.

'It's a tableau,' she explains. 'That is the tree I always wanted to climb when I was seven or so. I have this leg problem—hip dysplasia—and surgery didn't quite work, so tree climbing wasn't in the cards. But I could see this tree from the attic window of the house where my mother worked. I imagined what it would be like to climb it, what I might find, how it might feel to be up so high, so close to the nest.'

'You did this yourself, the painting ...'

She nods.

'Plus moulded bits from feathers, clay and plastic. Bits and bobs. It's surprising what people throw away. What one can find.'

She pulls a large book—*Art of the Renaissance*—off the counter and places it on his lap. It's got some weight, but lacks the heft of a thick book of art.

'Open it,' she says.

He flips open the cover. The book has been hollowed out and he is inside a woman's room—feminine, but almost like a bordello with its deep red velvet bed curtains and bedspread. On top of the bed sit queer, minutely rendered stuffed animals. He peers more closely. The stuffed creatures are goblins, like something out of a Goya etching: sharp teeth, pointed ears. A trio of them writhe on the bed, looking as if they might leap up at any moment and dig their claws into his face. Adjacent to the bed is a black art deco vanity covered in a mess of spilled face powder and rouge, open lipsticks and nail varnish. A chartreuse vase overflows with once-sensuous pink Chinese peonies, now half-dead but still emitting a racy scent. Reflected in the vanity's mirror is a young woman, perhaps in her mid-twenties, with glossy dark hair and a bruised-looking face, furrowed brow. Her peacock-blue kimono is half-open, revealing cleavage, her soft stomach and wiry pubic hair. It could be Maria, he thinks, a younger version. In one hand, the woman holds a pack of Tarot cards, with the other she shows him the Devil.

The Devil. That can't be good, he thinks.

'It's so detailed,' he whispers. 'These are shadow boxes?'

He's read about them. They were popular in the nineteenth century and some survive in museum collections. Mostly they were collages of natural wonders—collections of shells and coral depicting underwater life or butterflies in their habitat—whereas this depicts the interior, the domestic.

'This is what might have been if I'd continued on my path when I was younger,' she says. 'I was a vain thing. The demons—jealousy, vanity and sexual wantonness—hounded me. If I hadn't changed, this is what I might have become.'

'We all have demons,' he says. 'It took me years to see mine: I'm a perfectionist. I wish I'd seen it sooner.' Then Gabby might have stayed, he thinks, completing the sentence in his head. He reddens, realizes he's said too much, has teetered on the brink of being unprofessional, has perhaps actually fallen into the turbulent waters.

'Are there more?' he asks, to deflect attention from his slip.

She nods, sweeps her arm around the room.

'All part of the main exhibit,' she says.

'Exhibit?'

'In The Museum of Possibilities.'

He looks around, suddenly seeing the order beneath the oppressive quantity of objects. Strata emerge: books stacked, relatively symmetrically, at the bottom, topped by the larger boxes, then smaller shoeboxes and the like on top of them. He wonders why he didn't see this arrangement before.

He is accustomed to the homes of hoarders: piles with no logic, random as a lottery. Boxes of broken crayons. A bag containing a new cardigan, tags still attached, the receipt indicating it was purchased five years earlier. A half-dozen jugs of bleach, marked down to ninety-nine cents each. Sacks of cat food, though there is no cat, and perhaps never has been. Bags and bags and bags. There is nothing like that in Maria's apartment.

'Would you like that cup of tea now?' she asks.

He glances at his watch. Time is up, but it's nearly lunch hour, his own time.

'Yes, please, if you don't mind,' he says.

Todd watches as she moves through the kitchen, graceful, precise. She fills a red kettle, measures loose tea into a worn gold-patterned teapot, sets out mismatched cups and saucers. Despite the state of her floors, she is not the sort of person to use a mug. There is something elegant about her, something attractive under the baggy black sweater. Perhaps I'm remembering the image in the box, he thinks.

'You've lived here, what, twenty years?' he says.

'Twenty-one, well, close to twenty-two. I never thought I'd stay. It was supposed to be temporary. I was looking for work, putting another life behind me. I did find work'—she nods her head toward the living room—'just not the paying kind.'

'What did you do before?'

'Ah, this and that. Mostly my grandfather's business.'

'In what field?'

'Taxidermy.'

'Taxidermy?' he says. 'I didn't think that still existed. Why did you leave?'

'It's a long story. I'll tell you another time,' she says.

'I'm not supposed to come back,' he says.

'I know. You mentioned a young woman. I won't let her in,' she says, meeting his eyes as she hands him his cup and saucer.

'So what would you suggest?' he asks.

She blows softly on the liquid in her cup.

'It's up to you,' she says.

He's about to say it isn't when he realizes she's right. What harm can one more visit do? What are they going to do, he thinks, fire me?

'One more visit then. Tomorrow,' he says. 'Ten okay?'

She nods.

On his way to the parkade, he realizes he's forgotten his umbrella. It's stopped raining now and he can't be bothered returning to fetch it. I'll be back tomorrow, he thinks.

———————

Is she insane? he wonders as he walks from the parkade back down her tired street. She is a bit. It's hard to know for sure, he thinks. What normal person would choose to live in such a tip? And he hasn't even seen the bedroom. That's usually the worst. Even an artsy type wouldn't live like that. An artist. The word alarms him. Is that what she is? He's met them before in his line of work, but she doesn't fit the type. They were loud-mouthed, flamboyant dressers, always trying to promote their work and castigating him for shackling their alleged creativity.

He recalls a woman saying to him: One cannot make anything

worthwhile when one is caught in a web of conventionality. He told her she was being a prima donna at the state's expense and completed the requisite Clean Sweep paperwork with gusto. Mostly he was incensed at her assumption that because he works for Social Services, the government, he couldn't possibly understand creativity or art. Her implication was that he had lost his soul, or rather sold it for that velvet coffin: a comfortable pension with full benefits. It's true that he is now counting the days until he retires, but he wasn't always that way. He had once found satisfaction in his work. And he has always nurtured his love of art, especially since Gabby left. These days he spends his evenings attending public lectures and gallery openings where he sips tangy red wine and peers at the pictures, but never dares to engage anyone in conversation. He reads books from the library: real books—battered now, but with beautiful illustrations—not those poor-resolution digital versions. He has a few good-quality prints at home and one lithograph of Ernst Haeckel's sea anemones, quite rare, which he inherited from his grandfather. It hangs in the place of honour above the gas fireplace.

Under the hostile glare of unexpected sunshine, the apartment building looks even more weather-beaten. Garbage has supplanted flowers in the meagre beds, nesting around the base of gangly hydrangea. Graffiti—a rust-red tag—scars the panel beside the front door. Inside, he notices that the mailboxes have all been pried open, all in various stages of becoming unhinged. He's determined to get down to business with Mrs Petali, to sort out the artworks, if that's what they are, from the rest. It's in her best interest, he thinks. He considers it a professional challenge. Better me than those yobs from Clean Sweep.

———

He totes a knapsack filled with black plastic garbage bags for trash, clear bags for stuff to be given away, plus box cutters and duct tape. It's a Portable Start-Up Kit 659 that he pilfered from the Mini Sweepers' supply cabinet. He thinks about the job ahead. All those boxes and books; they can't all be what she says. If I can get her started, she might agree to let one of the Mini Sweepers—minimum-wage pensioners mostly—help her sort things. But he suspects this conventional strategy won't work; hers is hardly a conventional case. He's not sure it's a case at all. He hasn't yet filed Home Visit Form XTP34.

Maria answers the door as he knocks, as though she was waiting on the other side. Her dark hair is woven into a single braid that hangs over one shoulder. She wears a snug-fitting black ballet top and gold hoop earrings. Good signs that she's caring for herself, he thinks professionally. And she looks so much younger, almost attractive.

'Mrs Petali …'

'Maria,' she says. 'There's tea and I've prepared a small exhibit for you.'

'But Mrs Petali, Maria, we really must get down to business. To sorting. Better us than the others.'

'This won't take a minute,' she says.

She turns and limps down the hallway. He hesitates, then follows.

'Sit,' she says, indicating the chair from yesterday. She thrusts a cup and saucer into his hands. Tea with milk, as he prefers it. Yesterday she'd served it clear; there had been no offer of milk and he hadn't bothered asking.

He notices she's made room on the island for two boxes, shiny with advertising for a hands-free, three-in-one saw and a Glow-Brite microwave. As she opens the saw box, he finds himself holding his breath and leaning forward. Inside is a diorama of what appears to be a party. A tasteful invitation is tucked into the front corner:

You are cordially invited …

The type of party is not specified, but it's obviously under way. The action is focused on an old man in a close-fitting, coal-black suit. Too elderly to stand, he sits in a white, mid-century club chair, a style Todd has often admired but can't afford. He holds a glass in his hand: martini, two olives. The man looks familiar. Like my father, thinks Todd. Or Cousin Theo. But older of course, much older than Theo. Older than me, he thinks.

The guests lined up in front of the man are wearing ghoulish costumes: an executioner brandishing a blood-smeared axe; a heavily veiled, laughing widow showing off what looks like a human finger attached to a long chain around her neck; a tall, swarthy man in a stovepipe hat clutching a clipboard. In a corner of the room, a clutch of demons, like something from a Bosch painting: drooling, red-eyed, pointed talons digging into their neighbours' flesh. They leer at a stooped old woman whose long, coarse, grey hair covers her breasts and pubic area, yet otherwise leaves her naked. Folds of belly protrude through her hair. Her thighs are pocked with cellulite and her toenails are like claws. This aged Venus sneers at the demons; disdain, verging on hate, emanates from her vacant, black eyes.

'It's horrible,' he mutters, not knowing precisely what to say. 'So detailed ... so real.'

Maria shrugs.

'One learns such things, seeing what could be,' Maria says. 'Nothing is impossible. A wrong turn. An unfortunate friendship. A debt to the wrong person. A misunderstanding. Like the tableau we saw yesterday depicting my possible trajectory.'

She pauses as if waiting for him to say something. He wants to ask for the backstory. Who is the man and what has he done? But he hesitates. What am I afraid of? he wonders. In the moment of his indecision she closes the box and prepares to open the second.

'Are you ready for more?' she asks.

These are addictive, he thinks, like chocolates. Not necessarily good for you, but irresistible. 'Of course,' he says.

She opens the second box, revealing an office in a handsomely proportioned room with floor-to-ceiling windows. Like one might find in Paris, Todd thinks. Framed in the window is a city of four- and five-storey buildings in grey stone, likewise with tall windows. In the centre of the room, a man sits at an expansive teak desk, the kind Todd has always admired, but at the same time holds in disdain for taking up so much space. The man is gazing out the window, his face half-averted.

On the wall hangs a Modigliani print. Todd recognizes it from a trip he made with Gabby to Paris, his first and only trip abroad. The trip had been her idea, ostensibly to look at art, but actually an unstated attempt to rekindle their marriage. He didn't think Gabby would enjoy going through galleries and museums day after day, but she proved to match his enthusiasm. She even suggested that he return to school to study art history. He laughed, said it was preposterous. What would he do with such knowledge? He remembers they almost bought a print of this very Modigliani. A portrait of his partner, Jeanne Hébuterne, eyes open, her hand on her shoulder. In the gift shop they had both admired the image, but when he went to order it from the clerk, he asked for 'Jeanne Hébuterne with a Yellow Sweater' instead. In it, Jeanne's eyes are black ovals, blank. He and Gabby quarrelled about it afterward. She couldn't understand why he'd suddenly changed his mind when it was all settled. She felt slighted, ignored. He refused to justify his change of heart. It was narratives such as these that severed them in the end. He knows this now.

He doesn't mention this trip to Maria. Why would he? He decides that the picture in the tableau is a coincidence, nothing more.

Other paintings also adorn the walls; he doesn't recognize the works per se, yet the artists seem familiar. A Picasso perhaps. Maybe a Monet. An early Richter. What space is not taken up by paintings is dominated by floor-to-ceiling oak bookshelves loaded with large art books, punctuated periodically by sculptures and ceramic works. He recognizes three of Jim Thomson's famous sieves.

'What the hell...?' he murmurs to himself.

His eyes turn again to the man in the chair. He seems more visible now, as if he has half-turned toward Todd, but of course that's impossible. The man is distinguished, almost handsome, with a trim grey-and-white beard, closely tailored clothes and gold cufflinks in his fine cotton shirt. He is balding, not unlike Todd. In fact ... Todd peers more closely. There is a resemblance. More than his father or his cousin Theo.

It's intended to be me, he realizes. My possible life? It's preposterous!

'It's a possibility, or it was at one time,' says Maria, as if reading his thoughts. 'Different choices. Different paths chosen,' she continues. 'Not social work but business, art history. It would have required awareness at an earlier age, a chance encounter perhaps, a different upbringing. Some possibilities arise because of the choices we make, others out of circumstances beyond our control. Either way they are latently present—our potential realities.'

'It's impossible,' he says, a note of hostility in his voice.

'Yes and no. There's little you could have done to ensure it.'

'What does he do for a living?'

'A dealer in art. Respected, renowned. Able to spot fakes easily, in people and in works. A wise man.'

He looks again and sees, to the side, a woman who can only be Gabby: lithe, blond French twist, elegant reading glasses balanced on her nose as she bends intently over an art book.

'It's not,' he mutters.

He doesn't want to deal with this. He glances at his watch; the hour's nearly up. 'Mrs Petali,' he says, 'we must make some headway. Surely there is something you can part with among all this. . . .'

She looks at him, slowly closes the tableau.

'Some of the boxes are empty,' she says reluctantly. 'But they're for future projects.'

'You can get other boxes.'

'But these are perfect,' she mutters.

'We have to start somewhere,' he insists.

She hands him one box at a time, and he collapses them with his box cutters and duct tapes them together. There are fourteen in all. Barely a dent in the debris, he thinks.

'Surely there are other things,' he says. 'Or perhaps you can clean and put away the pots and pans.'

'Oh, they aren't for cooking. I make the rubber, resins. Those are the smells that people complained about, but I make sure to open the windows now.'

'And the cupboards?' he asks.

She flips one open. It's filled with paint and brushes, paper, cardboard: the tools of her trade.

Is she a genius or insane? he wonders again

He persuades her to toss some of the tubes of dried glue, nearly empty tins of paint—decades old, judging by the prices. He tries to appeal to her logic.

'If you can clear the counter,' he says as he leaves, 'we could make some real progress.'

'You don't understand,' she says. 'I thought you would.'

'I do, I do. They're so realistic, but Mrs Petali, we must be practical.'

'I am practical,' she snaps. 'You see the possibilities I've considered. What you are talking about—clearing it all away—it's impossible for me. This is my life's work.'

He glances at his watch. Despite himself, he feels a pang of sympathy for her, a recognition of her art.

'I can't stay any longer,' he says. 'I should send Sarah tomorrow, but I'll come during my lunch hour. We can talk some more if you like, but...'

She says nothing; there is nothing more to be said. As he leaves, she silently hands him the umbrella he'd forgotten the day before and presses the door shut behind him.

What more could I do? he thinks as he shuffles down the corridor. Still, he feels he's let her down.

Back at the office, he leafs through the requisite paperwork. It could get lost. I could dump the electronic records, he thinks. Shred the paper trail. It would be months before anyone caught on, at least as long as she continued to keep the apartment building hallway clear and the smells at bay. In any case, I'll be long retired if they ever trace it back to me. But why should I? he wonders. Her and her assumptions. She knows nothing about me. He thinks of the party tableau and wonders if she's some sort of sorcerer. And a highfalutin art dealer? With Gabby as secretary or assistant? It's preposterous. She's gone too far with her mumbo-jumbo. How could she know of my interest in art? Or of Gabby? Has she been spying on me? He feels anger rising at the presumptuousness of it, of her. Making things up so that hardworking people like me feel bad about who they are. What right does she have? What is she suggesting? That if only I had worked harder ...

He signs his name with a flourish on the Clean Sweep requisition. They'll come tomorrow at three p.m. They're never late.

———————

At noon, as promised, he knocks three times on the door. He hasn't brought any gear. No black bags, only the dossier. He's there ... he doesn't know exactly why he's there. Because I said I would be, is how he justifies it. He was up most of the night thinking about her, first discounting her and her work, then wondering if he'd done the right thing in scheduling the Clean Sweep crew. Then justifying it all over again. Then admitting that she got him right—or at least his dreams. It frightens and depresses him, but mostly, it threatens the scant control he has over his limited life.

He knocks again.

'Mrs Petali,' he calls, 'it's me, Mr Grimshaw.'

He waits, growing impatient, then angry. How dare she stand me up? he thinks. No matter, he has the dossier, which contains SS Document 613 A4: Permission to Enter. He goes to the super, who looks as though he's just woken up; his breath is ferocious, his hair stands on end. The super unlocks the door and is obviously curious to enter, but Todd dismisses him. He waits until the man has shuffled down the hallway, disappeared down the stairwell. These people, he thinks with exasperation. Voyeurs. Just nosy. He opens the door.

Everything is gone.

He hurries down the empty hallway to the kitchen, living room. Nothing. The boxes, the books—all gone.

'What the hell?' he mutters.

He hurries back down the hall, flings the bedroom door open. It, too, is empty, except for a single box in the middle of the floor. As he bends to pick it up, it falls open, startling him. He peers inside, then slumps to the floor. He begins to weep. He should have done more. He shouldn't have signed the form.

Inside the box is her empty living room; hanging from the light fixture, a rope; dangling from the rope, a woman: Mrs Petali. Maria. And off to the side, a male figure, clipboard in hand. His own face stares back at him.

LUCID
DREAMING

Clarisse enters the dream session as Mona hurries down the cold hallway to her daughter's nursery. A thin winter light strains through the narrow hall window.

Mona is wondering why her baby didn't wake up for her two a.m. feeding. They grow so quickly, she thinks. Sleeping through the night already. Only three months old.

Mona sweeps past Clarisse; she hasn't seen her yet. She reaches into the crib, laying her hand on the tiny shoulder, whispering:

— Katie, love ...

A gentle squeeze and another. Nothing.

— Katie, wake up. Wake up, she says, louder this time.

Mona lifts her limp daughter into her arms and comes to the unspeakable realization. Fresh, fresh, every time fresh hell ... A squeezing in her chest. A tide of tears plunging into a wave of grief. She clutches her daughter, collapses into her rocking chair, once a place of comfort and sweetness, a place to breastfeed her little Katie.

Clarisse sees that it is time to intervene. She puts her hand on Mona's shoulder. So much hinges on these moments, Clarisse reminds herself. Peace of mind, mostly.

— It's not your fault, Clarisse whispers, adopting her best kindly therapist voice. There was nothing you could do, she adds.

Mona leans against Clarisse. A torrent of tears rushes down her face.

— Mona, you know it's not your fault, whispers Clarisse. It's sudden infant death syndrome. You did nothing wrong.

The phone rings, as it has during the previous dream sessions, as it had that night.

— You don't have to answer, says Clarisse gently. She knows it is Mona's husband, away on a business trip, checking in before setting off on his day's meetings.

— There's no need to answer, Clarisse repeats.

The decision belongs to Mona. It must be hers.

It rings again. And again. Mona gets up and walks to the hall, to her husband's desk in the foyer; she picks up the receiver.

— Hello, she says.

There is a pause. She puts the receiver down.

— Well done, says Clarisse, holding Mona's elbow. No matter what he says, it's not your fault. He's just looking for someone to blame because he feels guilty.

———————

The ebb and flow of grief and self-recrimination have persisted for two years. When Mona is awake, she almost believes that she's not to blame for Katie's death, that her philandering husband is wrong about her. She is almost ready to accept that version of her story. Almost.

Mona's guilt incites her recurring nightmare, the episodic memory in which she finds Katie and loses herself. Clarisse believes that in dreams, the past and present merge and the possibility of change may arise. Mona can't change the facts—Katie's death, her husband's phone call—but her reaction is malleable. Clarisse has found that feeling can mitigate what memory purports to know. As the client relives the memory in her dreams, Clarisse intervenes. She amends the script, introduces a more compassionate view of events, one that gives the client peace, even closure. Clarisse offers a way to make memory a part of life, not the focus.

Clarisse's colleagues tell her she is brave, fearless even, to delve into the subconscious this way, but in discussion forums, her peers criticize her techniques for being overly intrusive, even unethical. To her, all that matters is that they work.

And that they belong to her. In the early days she gave equal billing to her lab tech, Liam, who developed the technical apparatus that made her work possible. But the therapy was based on her ideas, and she—not

Liam—came up with the therapeutic methodology. These days, if she gives credit at all, it's a cursory nod to Dr Frederik van Eeden who, in 1913, coined the term 'lucid dreaming', a hybrid between sleep and wakefulness—asleep, technically, yet aware that you are dreaming.

Dreams often mirror turning points in patients' lives, the point at which their illness first became manifest, Clarisse explains in PowerPoint presentations at international psychiatric conferences. She explains how oneirocritic therapy can allow resolution. Oneirocritic: interpreter of dreams. She likes the sound of that. But her patients can't pronounce oneirocritic, much less remember what it means. They call it 'hope therapy'.

———————

Sois douce, be gentle, gentle: this is Clarisse's mantra as she approaches the lab that Thursday evening. If all goes as planned, she will mostly be a witness in this third dream session with Mona. If not, she is prepared to step in, to reinforce the alternate script. With empathy if need be, although that has never come naturally to her. It is something she has practised, learning to ask the pertinent questions and give the pat replies of reassurance.

She enters the lab. Liam is sitting at the control panel, fiddling with one of the dozens of dials and buttons. She doesn't say hello.

'What stage has Mona reached?' she asks, nodding toward the first of two anechoic chambers.

'She had trouble getting to sleep. Poor Mona,' Liam says, without lifting his head. 'But she's just about in REM.'

Rapid eye movement: such an inadequate term for the pivotal point in accessing episodic memory—autobiographical memory, as Clarisse writes in her scientific articles. *This is where we access our narratives. This is the place where we can change our feelings and perceptions.*

'How much time do I have?' asks Clarisse.

'Hard to say precisely. An hour and twenty minutes, maybe an hour and fifteen. That's her statistical average. But it's only been the two sessions. Hardly a robust sample.'

'Thank you, Dr Spock.'

Liam says nothing. Clarisse means it as a joke, a compliment even to what she sees as Liam's attempt at being scientific, though he only has his undergraduate degree. Liam has learned to ignore these jabs, to accept them as part of her prickly nature.

Clarisse perches on a rickety wooden stool as Liam applies the electrodes to her head and neck. She keeps her hair closely cut, unattractively so, to make sure the electrodes attach securely. The connecting gel is cold against the pale skin of her neck.

She's felt out of sorts all day, but can't figure out why. I should be happy, she thinks. I'm getting everything I want: a research chair at a major university. Staff. A lab. Without Liam, sure, but he can't possibly object, she thinks. There's no point in asking him to move, because he can't. Not with his custody arrangement. He'd never see his son. He knows that. Plus, this way I can hire clean: someone more educated, more connected. I can really go places. Patents, rather than research subjects. An institute.

I'm tired, she decides. She hadn't slept well the night before; the only time she truly gets a good night's rest is in the anechoic chamber. Around four that afternoon, she'd considered having a coffee, a shot of caffeine, but she wasn't sure of the timing.

Dream therapy is always tricky, but especially when she's overtired. She must hold a state of lucid dreaming, able to enter another person's dream and function without losing control to her own subconscious narrative. But lucid dreaming happens in REM and can quickly degenerate into the bizarre and emotional. She lost lucidity once, when she and Liam were developing the entry technique. Clarisse's dream world and the client's collided. Characters mingled and meshed. Clarisse's mother appeared—her Catholic, French-Canadian, four-foot-eleven mother— and began having wild sex with the client's husband. Dreams are an unstable place.

Since then, Liam has been careful to wake her at the first hint—the slightest alteration in REM, a minute acceleration in heart rate—that lucidity is waning. Clarisse resents the fact that she must trust him absolutely, that he's the one in control when she's working.

This is her life's work. It's her life, if truth be told. Relationships always seemed a distraction, especially romantic connections, though there was a colleague once who might have proven useful. But then it emerged that he wanted children. Clarisse made conscious choices early in her career about what she did and did not want.

'Nearly done,' says Liam.

Down to business, she thinks. In her head, she goes over the short-form notes—her prompt for recalling the client's trajectory: *36 y. o. female. Low self-esteem. History of abusive relationships. Twice married. Husband having affair. Daughter died at 3 months: probable SIDS. Agoraphobic. Prolonged grief disorder. DSM-VII #632.*

Third dream. Clarisse has seen the mother's anxiety over her baby girl—the terror, the sorrow, the damning phone call—repeated twice. Now the third. It's always three times, in her experience, before some degree of resolution occurs. That's the magical bit, Liam said when they were developing the technique. Typical, she'd thought at the time. He likely believes in fairies too.

'What stage is Mona in now?' Clarisse asks Liam.

'Three. Her delta waves are slow and steady. She's less than an hour away from REM. You'd best get in and settle.'

She enters the second anechoic chamber, once used by the music department for recording, but now, after a bit of interdepartmental wrangling, her domain. Clarisse prefers sleeping there these days; the soothing rush of air as it enters and leaves the room lulls her seamlessly into sleep. She removes her shoes and jacket, lies down on the firm single bed and pulls the sheet up to her chin, all the while mentally reviewing the clinical details of Mona's case. Liam plugs in the electrodes and leaves without his usual parting words: 'Sweet dreams.' He's out of sorts too, she thinks. I'll wait until tomorrow to tell him that I'm leaving. This decision calms her. She closes her eyes, waits for the gentle pulse that will push her past stages one and two, into delta waves and less than an hour from REM.

Liam pulls the door shut. I should lock her in, he thinks, then grimaces at the thought. That wouldn't do at all. The cleaners would only find her and I'd be out a job.

Jennifer, the department admin clerk, told him about Clarisse's plans late that afternoon. Liam knows that Jennifer has a crush on him, but she's too young and he's too busy with his son and besides, he works four nights a week; there's no time for socializing. Still, there's no harm in flirting. Jennifer had assumed, quite reasonably, that Liam already knew. She asked if he was moving with Clarisse, 'Professor Doucette'.

'I'm not exactly the big city type,' he'd said. 'And there's my son.'

He'd shown Jennifer photos of his five-year-old. His ex-wife has custody during the week—she and her new husband, the man she'd left the marriage for. Liam gets the boy every weekend. He keeps the door to the boy's room firmly shut weekdays.

'It seems unfair, Professor Doucette leaving you behind,' said Jennifer. 'It's as much yours as hers. You know, the sleep lab stuff.'

'She's the head of the program,' said Liam with a shrug.

'I guess ... but it's not on. And it's so soon, too. Next term. What's her rush?'

'Ah well,' he said, 'life's not often fair, is it, Jennifer?'

She smiled up at him, admiration gleaming in her heavily lined brown eyes, but his mind was already elsewhere.

Only a month, he thought. When exactly was she going to tell me? Fecking git! After all these years working together, pretending we were partners.... She could've at least asked me if I wanted to go, given me a chance to say no. Or maybe I could arrange something ... drive back here on weekends or something. What does she know?

He'd thought about confronting Clarisse, but he knew he'd lose his temper and then she'd have the upper hand—all cool and collected, per usual. Besides, he already knows the answer. The deal is struck and he's not part of it. She's headed for bigger things, leaving him to stew in this poky lab.

He stands in the cool control room, watching through the two-way mirror as Clarisse settles into sleep. *How can I go back to what this job used to be? Tedious third-rate experiments by wanna-be tenure-track researchers? It's bloody unfair. Jennifer's right. I'm the one who designed and built the equipment. Without me, Clarisse would have nothing. She would be nothing but another psychiatrist with a harebrained idea based on Freud or some other wanker.*

Then he remembers the manual: *I'm the wanker*, he thinks. *Last week, Clarisse asked him to pull together all the procedures, just in case he fell sick or got hit by a bus. In her dreams*, he thinks. *I'm a fecking eejit for giving it to her. But only a printout*, he thinks, *and just yesterday. She hasn't asked for the electronic version. Sure, she has pieces of info in emails and whatnot, but not the key bits. If I can get the manual back …* he thinks. *Well, without that she has nothing but a few theories. I'll do it now while she's in the chamber*, he thinks, *in case she decides to take it home. If she hasn't already.*

He goes back to the panel and looks at the brain waves. *Clarisse is ready for the push.* He gives the pulse and waits. Sure enough, she enters slow-wave. *There's time now*, he thinks. *Nearly an hour, give or take, before* REM.

He rummages in her purse, grabs her keys, then races up to her corner office on the third floor. He knows the cleaners are finished for the night; he knows all about the building's nocturnal life. He quietly closes her office door behind him and rifles through the papers on her desk, then scans the bookshelves. *It's not there.* He checks her key chain for the desk drawer key and clicks the drawer open. But no, it's not there either. *Maybe she took it out of the blue binder*, he thinks. *Maybe she put it in a file.* He sorts through the keys again, trying a couple before he can open the file cabinet. He begins going through the files, not so carefully this time, rummaging quickly, not stopping even at his own personnel folder. His heart drums in his chest; his mouth is dry.

He glances at his watch. It's all taken longer than he'd thought. *Bloody hell*, he thinks. He hurries back down to the lab, hoping Clarisse is still in lucid dreaming. There'll be hell to pay if she's floundering in REM.

Who cares? he thinks. She deserves what she gets.

———

Clarisse enters the dream session as Mona hurries down the cold hallway to her daughter's nursery. A thin winter light strains through the narrow hall window.

Mona wonders why her baby didn't wake up for her two a.m. feeding. They grow so quickly, she thinks. Sleeping through the night already. Only three months old.

Mona sweeps past Clarisse, not seeing her yet. She reaches into the crib, laying her hand on the tiny shoulder, whispering:

— Katie, love . . .

A gentle squeeze and another. Nothing.

— Katie, wake up. Wake up, she says, louder this time.

Mona lifts her limp daughter into her arms and comes to the unspeakable realization. Fresh, fresh, every time fresh hell . . . A squeezing in her chest. A tide of tears plunges into a wave of grief. She clutches her daughter, collapses into her rocking chair, once a place of comfort and sweetness, a place to breastfeed her little Katie.

Clarisse sees that it is time to intervene. She puts her hand on Mona's shoulder.

— It's not your fault, Clarisse whispers, adopting her best kindly therapist voice. There was nothing you could do, she adds.

Mona leans against Clarisse, a torrent of tears rushes down her face.

— Mona, you know it's not your fault, whispers Clarisse. It's sudden infant death syndrome. You did nothing wrong.

The phone rings, as it has during the previous dream sessions, as it had that night.

— You don't have to answer, says Clarisse gently. She knows it is Mona's husband, away on a business trip, checking in before setting off on his day's meetings.

— There's no need to answer, Clarisse repeats.

The decision belongs to Mona. It must be hers.

It rings again. And again. Mona rocks in her chair, her eyes fixed in front of her. Finally the ringing stops.

— Well done, says Clarisse. It's not your fault no matter what he says.

Mona stops rocking, she looks up at Clarisse.

— It's yours, she says. It's your fault. You were the only one here with Katie. What are you doing here? John! she calls. John?

Clarisse doesn't panic; such deviations aren't uncommon.

— I'm here to help, says Clarisse. My name is Dr Clarisse Doucette. You asked me to help you. Katie died of SIDS. You know that.

— John? calls Mona.

They hear heavy footsteps running down the hall. Clarisse feels her pulse pick up. John is volatile. And big. She and Mona both turn, but it's Liam who enters the nursery.

— Liam, thank goodness, says Clarisse.

— When were you going to tell me? Liam asks.

Abruptly, they are in the sleeping chamber of the lab. They're yanked out of Mona's dream world, into Clarisse's.

— I would have asked you to move with me, says Clarisse—but your son ... I didn't want to put you in conflict. I knew you wouldn't be able to come.

— You knew? You didn't even bloody ask! But you knew? You'd be nothing without me, says Liam, his black eyes riveted on her.

She feels her heart rate pump up.

— I would have asked, Liam, if I thought there was a chance.

Her palms are damp.

— No, you wouldn't have, says Liam. You never had any intention of bringing me along. Your little lab rat with the embarrassing credentials.

— No, that's. . . .

— You and your PhD. You're nothing but a thief. A common thief. I'm the one who knows how this works. I'm the one who developed the technical ability. You just had a lot of grand ideas on a piece of paper. They meant nothing until I found a way to make it happen. And now, now you think you can just walk away with all my ideas in your briefcase? It's not on. I won't allow it.

For once, Clarisse is speechless. He seems menacing to her. Meek Liam. She rushes to the door of the lab, turns the handle, but it's locked.

Let me out of here, Liam. You have no right . . .

Suddenly, he's somehow outside the sleeping chamber, standing at the control panel. He turns some dials, hits a switch.

A shock of pain pulses through her head.

Then there is white.

PLACES
WE CANNOT GO

I'm an understanding person, liberal-minded, but I can only take so much. That sounds insincere, doesn't it? Like some cliché a closet bigot would spout. I never thought I'd say it either, but then, I never thought Melanie would behave like this and expect us to stay friends.

Even when she told me she was gay, did I say anything negative? Was I repulsed? No, of course not. I was understanding. Whatever-makes-you-happy, I said. Truth is, though, I never believed she was gay. I thought it was a reaction to all her horrible experiences with men. Maybe she thought she could find more compassion with a woman. She had me, sure, but obviously that wasn't enough.

You have to understand about Mel. She needs to be *in* love. It comes to her easily—and quickly. A curse more than a blessing. Right away she's phoning the guy all the time, wanting to get together. Not everyone appreciates it.

Like the guitarist she fell for and slept with, all in one night. I'd told her a million times, it's always a mistake to hop into bed right away. I know men, I know what they want, how they're guided by their little pink head. Mel listens, nods, says I'm so wise, then ignores my advice. The next afternoon, for some inexplicable reason, she left a cactus at the guitarist's apartment door with a note saying that, like the cactus, she, too, was capable of blooming if properly nurtured. A strange thing, this prickly portent. Naturally he took it that way, too. Or maybe all he ever wanted was a one-night stand. Anyway, he never called her. And I heard all about it. For weeks she rehashed the evening, the beers (was it eight or nine?), the joints, the lovemaking. Me, reiterating the girlfriend platitude ad nauseam: 'He isn't worth it. He doesn't deserve you. You're so (insert appropriate new adjective-du-jour).'

Then there was the fellow in her painting class. 'Pete Picasso'—I can't remember his name. Melanie fell for him like a blind roofer. He was artistic, talented and bohemian—all the things she aspired to be. They started clubbing—pogoing to punk, swaying to reggae—and ended up sleeping together for a few weeks, toothbrushes duly deposited in each other's bathrooms. That was our agreed-upon sign of a promising relationship—with a man, anyway, because I always had one at Mel's place, too. Then Pete, or whatever his name was, told her it was over, denied there was someone else though she'd seen him conferring over coffee with an SYT, our shorthand for sweet young thing. She moaned for weeks; I offered more girlfriend platitudes late into the night, then we sprawled together in her queen-sized bed. She fell asleep quickly and I would lie beside her, not touching, not quite, but close, so I could feel the warmth from her bare arms and legs. I would lie, hardly moving until I heard the birds wake in the park across the street, then I would succumb to a few dreamless hours of unconsciousness.

We were still in university at that time. I was in fourth-year English and working my butt off to graduate with top honours. No time for men. And after listening to Mel's stories for years, I'd decided they weren't worth the effort—their fragile egos needed continual bolstering and then, after you'd prostrated yourself by excessively complimenting and reassuring them, they bolted anyway. I knew before I started any relationship that I'd be left hating myself, hating them; it was a no-win game and the stakes were too high. Besides, Melanie was enough: fun, interesting, smart. Sure she was high-maintenance, what with her messy love life and seven a.m. phone calls, her mid-afternoon pleas for company, a beer and a smoke—'choke and a gargle' we called it. High maintenance, but she was so amusing, always had a long, shocking story to tell, always wanted to go places: art exhibits, the agricultural fair, a butterfly garden. And at least I knew she wouldn't break my heart.

Mel and I met in first year at the Black Swan, the university coffee house. I was drinking my habitual three p.m. apple juice and struggling to read Chaucer. Melanie was sipping green tea and eating a bran muffin. I'd never seen anyone eat a muffin the way she did: carefully tearing off bits, popping them one by one into her mouth. It seemed so decadent. Even the muffin itself, swollen and loaded with raisins, was foreign, exotic. You never saw stuff like that in Saskatoon, not in the late '70s. After eating the muffin, Melanie carefully wiped her hands on a cloth hanky, then started making notes about a book on Frida Kahlo. When her pen ran out of ink, she asked if I had a spare. We started talking, or rather she started talking about her courses in fine arts, tuition fees and, inevitably, her lacklustre love life. I listened. When it was time for my next class, she asked for my phone number and I was inexplicably thrilled. I asked for hers too, just in case she lost mine.

Unlike her would-be paramours, I phoned her back. We met the next day and the next, every day after that. We took long walks around the city, usually ending up at the Wheat Sheaf near Kensington Market, drinking glasses of forty-cent draft in a haze of smoke and ignoring the old men in stained pants who stared at us. Then we'd go, half-pissed, to some second-hand-clothing stores she knew, which I could never find when I was sober. We snagged coats for five bucks, lovely beaded cashmere sweaters for eight. This was before retro was in but she had second-hand shopping down to an art. We spent hours putting together her get-ups, right down to the underwear: cleavage-enhancing vintage bras, slips edged in black lace that contrasted with her pale skin and lightly freckled shoulders. My favourite outfit was her swirling red skirt, black ballerina top, black patent flats and dangling jet earrings. She'd put her hair in a snarled upsweep with a red scarf and it somehow stayed put. I don't know how she pulled it off, but she always looked great even though she's not what you'd call good-looking; her eyes are close set and her nose is too big. She's interesting—that's it. She looks interesting. And sexy too, but not in that predictable, air-brushed, *Playboy* way.

I began dressing in a pale imitation of her, trading my jeans and

T-shirts for peg-leg men's pants, dress shirts and narrow '40s ties. A little butch, I admit, but practical. And good for warding off men, pre-empting potential advances, though that seemed increasingly unlikely.

Of course, that was all a long time ago. I'd never had a girlfriend like her before. Mel was so exotic in her strangely beautiful clothes, turning heads everywhere she went, and she could talk about anything: Frederick's of Hollywood lingerie, Walker Evans's Depression photography, postwar Danish teak furniture. She knew all about art and style, but she never made me feel like a prairie-town dweeb—even though I was. Probably still am.

It was difficult for me when I first moved to Toronto; the constant hum of traffic kept me awake for hours. I'd walk the streets, looking at people's faces, looking for someone I knew. I developed routines to settle me: buy groceries Friday at six, apple juice at the Black Swan every afternoon at three; laundromat Saturdays at eight a.m. before the rush. It settled me, but it didn't lift my loneliness.

Then Melanie swept me into her life.

She told me about her father in Boston who never really lived with them; I met her mother, whose whole life is high drama. Going for milk at the corner store once ended in international subterfuge following her mother's encounter with a charming but demanding Iranian who wanted help getting his family to Canada. Another time, she met an elderly Bay Street businessman on the subway who invited her for lunch, where he proposed a ménage à trois with his wife. I don't know how Mel's mom does it, attracting this kind of attention. The large bosom helps. And it is a bosom, like a box on her chest. Breasts bound together in some strapped corset thing, like a straitjacket. Mel and I used to laugh at her mother's foibles, but she's a wonderful woman.

And Mel? Mel said she felt like she'd found a sister in me. I readily agreed, but in my heart I wondered: Were sisters so close? Did they tell each other everything? Weren't they competitive, at least for their parents' affections? Mel was my best friend, my confidante, the one person I knew I could always count on. But to me, we were more than friends or even sisters. We were intimates. I didn't tell Mel how I felt. There didn't seem to be any point. She wanted a sister and decided I fit that role. I think it's because we are both only children with one parent. She has her mom, I have Dad.

Mel met him way back then, too. Dad used to fly in from Saskatoon for conferences and symposia on bioethics and placebo use in clinical trials or some such. He'd take us out for dinner at Barberian's and we'd finger the crisp linen tablecloth as we ate the biggest steaks on the menu. Starving students, he'd laugh. He's such a sweet man, though he doesn't talk much. He's probably all talked-out from lecturing. He always asked if I needed anything, and he was quick and generous with the cheque-book, but he's at a loss with young women—with women in general. He never dated after Mom died, though well-meaning friends were always trying to match him up during meticulously plotted dinner parties. He fails to impress. Sort of like me, I guess. But with Mel I didn't have to worry about that. She thought I was great just the way I was.

I don't know what she thinks now.

The problem was a man. That's always been Mel's problem. You see, she's the kind of woman who really needs a guy, if you know what I mean. I don't even think about men anymore. I was content to be Mel's friend and I think I was pretty good at it: loving, helpful, not critical. We'd been friends for six, nearly seven years. We graduated from university and each rented a tiny bachelor apartment, which we spent months furnishing with findings from junk stores and auctions. I became a junior editor at Pigeon Publishing, ransacking towering piles of manuscripts, reading them on the subway, in the bathtub—hoping to find that one good author who would establish my reputation. It was mostly crap, though I did get a few titles on our list. I had no time for men. Melanie found a co-op studio space and started painting, but she still dated—and was dumped.

I tried to tell her that she went for the wrong sort of guys. Artsy types with no stability. Guys who fall in love as easily as an orgasm, fall out of love as simply as shutting a door. Guys who leave you waiting outside an art theatre in minus thirty. Guys who make promises they never keep. Guys who live in hazardously messy apartments and talk endlessly about creative potentiality instead of living it. I know the type. After Melanie? Whoa, do I know the type. We'll travel, they say. I'll introduce you to the owner of Gallery 222. I'll buy you that book on O'Keeffe and Stieglitz. And they never do.

Not like me. I kept my promises, bought her books and costume jewellery, treated her to movies and dinners at modest cafés. She was always so appreciative.

Then she met someone—Joe—who she swore was the one. But suddenly she was stingy with the details. They went to a club on Saturday night, sure, but which one? And what did he say? What did he do?

Two weeks in, she invited me over for dinner and I knew she was going to tell all. She made pizza dough with whole-wheat flour and water. No yeast, because she's heard it gives you yeast infections, which is probably bullshit but I didn't say anything. It doesn't matter. She topped it with feta cheese, because mozzarella is fattening. All the while, not a word about the new man in her life. Dinner wasn't ready until nine and by then I could have eaten cardboard. Just as well because the crust was exactly like cardboard, but at least the veggies and cheese were good. Finally, Melanie said she had something to tell me.

An I-hope-you-aren't-shocked something.

She told me she had been dating a lesbian.

'I'm gay,' she said.

I hesitated. My heart fluttered then sank. I should have been happy for her, but instead … I nodded anyway, said, 'That's-wonderful-whatever-makes-you-happy.' I gave her a big hug and felt—not for the first time, but this time I noticed—her full breasts against my flat chest. I wondered what they did in bed together. If Mel was satisfied. With a woman.

Who knows though, maybe she was in love because Jo—short for

Joanne, it turns out—was a wonderful woman. Butch, sure. Not like Mel at all: cropped hair and practical Eddie Bauer clothes, sort of my style. But she had this hilarious deadpan sense of humour. Loved to gossip about her gay friends, their mishaps and relationships. Melanie said Jo had always been gay, but hadn't had much luck with women. She was great, but she didn't seem like Mel's type: not artsy or outlandish. I didn't think it would last.

Jo and Melanie moved into a small house on the edge of the Beaches. I'm sure it used to be a cottage; it's practically in the lake and the wind howls through the walls. Mel painted the rooms tropical colours: Sea Foam in the living room, Calypso Orange for the hallway, Sparkling Sun in the kitchen. She got a designer friend to help with the lights, each of which must have cost a week's groceries for a family of four. Jo paid. She's a financial consultant at some Bay Street company, earns a lot more than Mel or me. Mel still works part-time at the Korkok Gallery and at her art co-op near Dufferin Street, where her studio space is. She pays the bills, keeps the books and stuff. Plus she paints when she can. She doesn't earn much dough; Jo paid for almost everything. They bought retro '50s furniture—Mel's choice, of course—including a long, hard couch with no armrests and two rickety end tables. Well, to each her own. You hardly noticed the bad furniture anyway because Mel covered the walls with her enormous paintings.

Depictions of deceit. That's what we called them, Mel and I. The paintings show interior scenes. In every one, there's a person, off to the side, partially hidden, peeking, seeing, listening to what they shouldn't. And what they shouldn't be seeing takes up most of the canvas: lovers beneath red silk sheets; a student peeking at her neighbour's test; a girl snooping through her mother's bureau. Mel laughed at their antics, said they epitomized the human penchant for deception—most often self-deception. You could see these characters as benign, but to me—the cheaters, the thief, the snoop—they were filled with malice, intent on fulfilling their own desires without thought for anyone else. Not that I ever said that to Mel. After all, she's the artist, she knows what they're about. I often wondered why Mel never asked me to pose for her. I imagined myself nude, in front of her, modestly holding a towel in front of my pubic hair. I wanted her to paint me, but I never dared ask. She's so talented. The works are loaded with details: shimmering tapestries, tight expressions and telling gestures. Not that I'm an expert or anything, but I do think they're fantastic and I don't understand why they don't sell better. In the two and a half years she's been painting them, she's only sold three. I couldn't afford one, but I bought another piece, way back in the day: a picture of Canova's statue 'The Three Graces', posed in the Wheat Sheaf drinking glasses of draft. It's hilarious.

Anyway, this whole time while Mel and Jo were living together, Mel's mom never knew. As far as she was concerned, they were just roommates. For Mel, it was easier that way because who knows how her mom would have reacted. Hysterically? Stoically? It was a toss-up.

They seemed happy, Mel and Jo, and I was glad for them, I really was. Mel deserved stability, a real home. Still, I knew Mel. I was on the alert for the inevitable: the signs of the breakup. And inevitably they came.

'Jo's a slob. That's all there is to it.'

Mel's meticulous, everything in its place, gewgaws always dusted, always placed just so. Jo is the exact opposite. Her dresser top is heaped with junk, her clothes are piled on a chair. She leaves a trail of debris everywhere she goes in the house.

'Jo won't go out clubbing anymore.'

I didn't understand this. I love going out with Melanie; something interesting always happens.

I tried to be a good friend, though I have to admit my heart wasn't in it. I encouraged Mel to tell Jo how she was feeling, to get counselling—all that stuff you read about in those mags like *Cosmopolitan* that Mel's mom buys. 'Repairing rifts in your relationship'—you've got to love those titles. A couple of times Mel and Jo went to some new-age pseudo relationship counsellor who prescribed candlelit dinners and long walks. Nothing really changed but Mel seemed to settle down, started painting a lot again. And we started seeing more of each other, holding hands at scary movies, drinking beer and bowling, eating out. It was great to spend more time with her.

Then, in September, everything changed again. Mel discovered she had a half-brother. Her mom was seventeen when Gary was born; she put him up for adoption and told no one. Decades later, Gary tracked down Mel's mom and wrote her a letter. She wasn't keen to reply. She actually managed to contain her hysteria for a week before telling Mel about the letter. She said she wouldn't answer it, said it was better to let things go on as they were, that Gary would only resent her for giving him up. But Mel wouldn't hear of it. Many tears ensued. Mel argued that Gary obviously wanted to meet his mother and didn't she owe him that much? And besides—the clincher—she'd always wanted a big brother, even a half-brother. More than anything, I think it was curiosity that drove them: Did he look like them? What did he do? Was he rich? What were his adoptive parents like?

They arranged to meet at Mel's for lunch; her mom almost had a coronary while waiting. I got the blow-by-blow afterward. 'He's gorgeous,' Mel gushed. 'You'll have to meet him.' Gorgeous, and nice, too. Kind to Mel's mom—his mom. He told her he'd waited for this day for so long, played it over and over in his mind. 'You're just as I imagined,' he said. And Mel's mom relaxed a bit, told him about her job as an office administrator in public health.

Gary was an art teacher at the local college who did performance pieces at festivals across North America and installations—you know, found objects and stuff—at local galleries. They had several friends in common; it seemed incredible that they'd never met before.

Mel had found a new best friend. After that, she started seriously dissing Jo: she's neurotic about money, she yells at me, she snores. Whatever. And all my talk about counselling and stuff—well, Mel just wasn't open to it. If the spark is gone … she said. She started seeing more and more of Gary: going to arty movies, theatres, galleries, driving around the country picking up junk for his installations. Always just the two of them. She never invited me—though I love rummaging through second-hand stuff. A couple of times they included Jo but Mel said she complained afterward that Mel and Gary ignored her—giggled and whispered to each other. Mel said Jo made a BIG SCENE about it, said Gary and Mel were rude. Yelled it, according to Mel, though knowing Jo that seems unlikely. I asked Mel why she didn't stand up to Jo. She said she just wanted peace at home, didn't want to be squabbling all the time.

I figured that Jo was jealous of Gary. Hell, I didn't blame her—I was jealous too. All those outings with him were really cutting into my Mel time. Not that she's my only friend or anything. There's Erin at work, and my neighbour, Debra. But they're not Mel. I missed her. We knew each other so well, completed each other's sentences, spent hours talking about her relationships, art and family. We lent each other the books we read so we could talk about them. She always took me shopping, wanted my opinion on the clothes she tried on. I looked forward to seeing her, shaped my calendar around our outings. But after Gary came on the scene my calendar was practically empty.

Christmas came. Mel wanted to invite Gary and her mother over for the day but Jo said she wanted to have her gay gal-pals to the house like usual. There was a big fight and Mel eventually caved, said she'd have Christmas dinner with her family at her mother's apartment in Bloor Village. Mel wasn't happy about the arrangement because her mom's apartment is shabby and small and in a perpetual state of squalor. Every surface is stacked with magazines and other junk: cat toys, free samples of shampoo, extra toilet paper and sanitary pads still in plastic bags, the receipts dating back years. The place also reeks of cats—six in a one-bedroom apartment. I don't know why they didn't go to Gary's place instead. Maybe Mel wanted to play hostess to their new relative. Anyway, Mel went to work on her mom's place, threw out sixteen black garbage bags full of junk and recycled endless boxes of newspapers and magazines. She squabbled daily with her mom over what to keep, what to toss. Mel was relentless—justifiably so.

I went over the Saturday before Christmas to help paint the living room and I couldn't believe the difference. The place was borderline spartan. Even the cat smell was under control. Mel let her Mom pick the paint colour—though she went along to give advice. It's not what I would have picked. Pink Harmony it was called. It was meant to go with the oyster-coloured brocade couch that Mel spent two hours vacuuming and shampooing.

Mel was in high spirits, laughing, joking, excited about the Christmas party—even if it wasn't going to be in her home—and a little apprehensive. The living room is small so it didn't take long to paint. The colour was perfect: illuminating, but not glaring. Then Mel and I went out to get a small tree. We set out arm-in-arm down Bloor Street. The sun was nearly down and the car headlights winked as they passed. It was cool, no slush, but not cold. The air was still. We stopped for coffee at Hurricane's. We used to go there way back in our university days. We'd pop in to rehash the evening's hijinks—her mother's latest dramatics. Mel had hot chocolate—always did. I had cappuccino with low-fat milk. 'I'll watch my waistline even if no one else does,' I said. An old joke, but Mel grinned anyway.

'I want to tell you something,' she said, licking the chocolate off her plastic stir stick.

I prepared myself for her to announce she was leaving Jo.

Mel stirred her chocolate.

'But I don't know if I should,' she added. 'I don't know if I should tell anyone.' She licked the stick again.

So it wasn't Jo.

'Mel, you know you can trust me.'

'It's about Gary. And me. About us. This absolutely cannot be repeated. Not ever. Promise?'

I promised.

And so, I can't tell you what Melanie said—but I can tell you that I won't see her any more. I made up an excuse right then and left her in the pub. I won't be phoning her. Our friendship, or whatever it was, is over.

Though I don't know what I'll do now, without my Mel. It seems she did break my heart after all.

I'm a liberal thinker, but there are boundaries. There are places we cannot go, no matter what our hearts desire.

BURDEN
OF ANXIETY

Althea takes care of her hands, slathering them with thick, medicinal-smelling cream and encasing them in white cotton gloves every night, just as her great-grandmother had fifty years before. But Althea's reasons are not social.

She practises the ancient art of massage. Gentle effleurage, hand stroking, feather-light down the length of the back. Wringing, cupping. Pressing. Releasing harm, dispensing comfort.

This will be Sarah's second visit. At the first, Althea was astounded by her physical beauty: her perfectly proportioned body; her skin, flawless, nourished. Sarah said the massage was for pleasure, but Althea quickly felt the real reasons in Sarah's neck and back. Even after an hour of massage the muscles remained taut as a bowstring. The natural curves, the kyphosis, between the shoulder blades, and the lordotic, at the neck and small of the back, had all vanished under the burden of her anxiety. Her back was rigid, tense.

I will release that tension today. I will. Release that tension today, Althea repeats to herself. She finds an affirmation always helps. She drains her morning cup of chai, noting the twitch in her hands, their impatience to begin.

There is a long waiting list to get under those hands. Clients come from as far away as Toronto. Althea allows a full ninety minutes per visit, with half an hour in between. She refuses to go any faster because it's important to her to give her full attention. She doesn't want to cheat them. Or herself.

As she lights scented candles around the table, Althea notices that her hands are shaking. Twitching isn't unusual—like bored children in a doctor's waiting room—but this shaking is strange.

There is a tentative tap at the door. Sarah is dressed, almost swaddled, in a dull grey dress that muddies her already clouded blue eyes. Althea can see Sarah working her jaw, grinding her teeth, as they sit to chat beforehand.

'How are you feeling, Sarah?' she asks in her best soothing-masseuse voice.

'Fine,' says Sarah, smiling falsely.

'Are you still having trouble sleeping?' asks Althea, glancing up from her notebook. She watches Sarah's jaw grind rhythmically.

'Just the usual. Sometimes I wake up at about three and I can't get back to sleep. I'm thinking about going back to work, but I'm worried about not being able to look after the house.'

'Oh, we all manage,' says Althea, smiling. 'Who cares about the dust bunnies?'

Sarah does not smile.

Althea asks whether Sarah is using the relaxation podcast she'd emailed to her (she hasn't got the time, she says) and whether she is still getting headaches.

'Sometimes they knock me down,' says Sarah quietly.

Althea stops writing and looks up. She notices Sarah's efforts to conceal the deep circles under her eyes with makeup.

'I mean I have to sit down,' says Sarah quickly. 'And the pain just comes.'

'When?' asks Althea. 'Is there a particular time or event? A trigger?'

'Always after Armand and I have quarrelled.' Sarah whispers so softly that Althea has to lean in to hear.

Althea's right hand begins to shake again. She doesn't know much about Armand, except that he's a bigwig businessman in town, owns the car dealership on Highway 17.

'I'd rather not talk about it,' says Sarah.

Althea decides to use her best almond oil, lightly scented with orange blossoms. She rubs her hands together with the oil, warming up like a musician. She looks at Sarah's beautiful back and shakes her head: it's all wrong.

'I think we'll start with the neck and shoulders,' says Althea.

Her hands lightly feather the shoulders, neck, back, gently, stimulating, then press slightly harder and fan out over the lower back. Palms, fingers moulded to the skin.

Sarah's shoulder muscles are hypertonic, a textbook case of scapulae, common in tense or frightened people.

The hands begin effleurage along the sides of Sarah's neck. They inch slowly, soothing down the spine, total contact. In a subconscious movement her thumbs begin petrissage, gently lifting, kneading the lumps and knots.

There is no conversation, no sound.

The hands press on Sarah's upper back, the shoulders. Press, release, spiral. On the shoulder blades she begins vibrating—a refined, precisely controlled movement.

Althea closes her eyes, feels something rising through her fingers. Success, she thinks.

It comes up strong, then stronger. The fingertips tingle and the hands begin to shake. Suddenly Althea feels very afraid—her hands jerk away.

How unprofessional, she admonishes herself. What am I afraid of? It's only my imagination. But she is breathing hard. She pours more almond oil into her cupped hand. It is a pretence really, a chance to take a break. Sarah's skin is perfect. It does not drink the oil, just takes hummingbird sips.

The hands are positioned at the base of Sarah's neck, gently now, smoothing a bit, adding some pressure and releasing. They begin the vibrations. It rises again, this feeling. Now it changes to anguish, then fear, uncertainty.

Althea is used to drawing out the negative, the tensions, but this is more immediate and powerful.

Althea concentrates on steadying her hands. Then she lets them go, lets them do what must be done. She must help Sarah with the pain. She cannot stop now. Althea feels the fear enter her arms. She feels it travel up, growing, yet she continues. Her arms tingle with fatigue, as if she has been working all day. Just as she decides that it is time to break the touch, the fear enters her shoulders and a spasm of pain travels down her back.

'No!' cries Sarah.

Althea's pain vanishes with the cry. She is exhausted.

Sarah's back has relaxed at last. Althea views its natural, beautiful contours—the kyphosis and lordotic—with satisfaction. She glances at the clock. The time is already up, and all she's done is the back and neck. But she is too done in.

She quietly closes the door behind Sarah, goes to her desk and sits. Her arms and hands hang limply beside the chair. It is an effort to move even one digit.

———

Althea sips her morning chai. She still feels a bit unsteady after Sarah. She had to cancel the rest of her appointments yesterday—something she hates to do, but she didn't have the energy to work any more. In the afternoon she slept two hours. She can't quite figure it out—the intense feeling, the awful fear, was so real. She'd consulted her textbooks, but they were no use. She decides to ask some colleagues. Maybe one of them has experienced something similar.

Althea scrolls online through the city newspaper as she sips her tea. A headline catches her attention: her town is mentioned, and a murder. A young woman was stabbed to death. She was the wife of a local businessman. Her name was Sarah.

THINGS
WE HOLD DEAR

She presses steadily on the accelerator, pushing through the blizzard. The windshield wipers cut a swath before the view is quickly obliterated. The car hood is shrouded in white. Underneath it's red, fire-engine red: her deliberate choice so the car will be visible as she moves, point A to point B. Red, a colour to warn and alarm, a choice to pre-empt a crash during these necessary times of transition. To be stuck, alone, in between destinations—to her, this would be disastrous.

The snow gets deeper, past the car's bumper. She thinks if she keeps moving she'll get through. It is in the moment of hesitation when the car can be caught in the drifts, pulled under. The key is to keep going forward, no matter how incrementally.

For her, the car is more than a vehicle to get from point A to point B. It is a way out of her domestic self, into other worlds—worlds her husband doesn't know and never asks about. These alternate worlds are where she lives: work, art, play. The world with him is one of hibernation, regeneration: a chrysalis.

I stop reading. It's a bit obvious, don't you think? It's not only the car that has to keep moving, it's her. She can't sit still for a moment. What a mug's game! I found that out ages ago. I know I'm a bit extreme, rarely leaving the apartment, or this chair, but for Chrissakes don't try to apply your DSM-V labels to me. I know that tome by heart. I'm not agoraphobic—I can go out if I want to. I just don't want to. I've spent my whole life listening to the whiners of the world, dissecting their so-called problems and trying to prod them into self-awareness, mindfulness. Now that's a mug's game. She's as bad as any of them, with the mindfulness of a gnat. See how intent she is on her destination? She knows where she's going better than where she is. What's her name anyway? The author could tell us.

The snow falls steadily. Large flakes, like confetti at that parade, she thinks, like in that photograph taken in New York City at the end of the Second World War. The famous photo by Alfred Eisenstaedt: a sailor holding a woman, low over the pavement and kissing her as she swoons—subjugated, uncomfortable, in pain even—in that awkward posture. He holds her forever in the frame, preventing her from falling, yet the cause of her potential fall. What is she thinking? That he might let her go? That she trusts him, a stranger, not to, in that fleeting moment of passion and release and relief at the end of something unspeakable, at the start of something new, though tainted by the past.

She has read that behind the nurse, half-hidden in the photograph, is another woman—the woman the sailor will marry. In fact, they were already dating when Eisenstaedt pressed the shutter. This duplicity doesn't surprise her. It confirms what she has come to believe: misrepresentation is an inevitable condition of monogamy. She loves that this narrative stems from a simple photograph. It's what enticed her to photography in the first place.

Where she is driving from no longer matters to her: she has left that behind. She is moving onward to point A, where her husband is undoubtedly asleep by now. This is a relief to her. There will be no unwelcome groping, only a light snore, a slight shifting as she cautiously enters the narrow double bed beside him.

I usually don't read short stories. I like a longer relationship with my fictional company. My nephew Stefan gave me this book. Fuel for your habit, Auntie, he said. After all the years I've spent listening to my patients tell their stories, Stefan thinks I'm addicted to narrative. Even if he's right, it's harmless enough. And a darn sight more stimulating than watching those interminable mini-series: upscale soap operas to divert the gentrified, stupefied masses. At least this has compelling subplots.

Though it's maddening, too. Does the woman have a name? And where's she com-
ing from? I'm sure it's a damn sight more interesting than home and her lacklustre
hubby. At least I no longer have to contend with living with someone, with the
inevitable boredom and pettiness that comes with overexposure. My life is calm, just
the way I like it. The view out my window—the suburban backyards—only
changes with the seasons. It feels like rain today, but that won't stop Stefan. He
promised to visit. I really should answer the door this time.

She passes the first neighbour's house. Jack is a kind man despite his
obsession with trapping small animals. Her husband allows him to set a
line in their forest, an arrangement made long before she arrived at point
A, at a time when her husband lived there alone and socialized with the
neighbours. A fellowship of lads: beers in the barn, that sort of thing. But
that was before. Now she fulfills her husband's scant need for social contact. A game of crib, perhaps—*fifteen-two, fifteen-four and a pair is six*—a
few words of small talk concerning the interminable domestic arranging.
No more is required, outside the bedroom.

She says nothing to her husband about the trapping. Jack checks the
line every day so the animals won't suffer—at least not for long. She asked
him once what he caught. Fox mostly, he said. Sometimes a badger or
weasel, and once or twice, a snow-white ermine, like the fur edging on
the queen's scarlet velvet cape, he explained. She liked that he told her this
detail, though she knew it already. Early every morning, Jack roars
through the valley on his Ski-Doo. She never hears him return. Perhaps
she has already left for point B, the one her husband knows: her small
framing shop on a side street in the nearby Ottawa Valley town.

Jack's house lurks behind the veil of snow. She glimpses the shrouded
light emanating from the porch. Jack always keeps the light on. She's not
sure why. To establish his presence in the wilderness? she wonders. Keep
the critters at bay? Is he afraid?

Soon she will reach the crest of the hill and then the car will coast
down despite the snow. She doesn't think of the upward climb at the bottom, on the other side of the gully. In spring, the swollen stream floods

the culvert and Jack lays planks across the flooded road. He removes them when the pools vanish, when they are reabsorbed into the earth along with tadpoles and mosquito larvae.

The snow is thick, relentless. She squints through the screen: Is it my imagination? she thinks. Is the snow coming up over the hood? It can't be! She hesitates a moment, her foot easing up on the gas, and in that moment, that second of uncertainty, she loses momentum. The car slows. She presses the accelerator again—but it is too late. The back wheels spin, the car pivots slightly toward the ditch. She lifts her foot off the accelerator. The car stops.

She has been stuck in ice, knows to rock gently: reverse, then forward, forward, then reverse. But this is not ice. It's deep snow, with an undertow that could suck in the tires. She tries once more, pressing the accelerator ever so slightly. The wheels spin, she feels the car pivot left. The ditch! She fears the car being embedded, tilting, falling, flipping. She stops pressing, turns the ignition off.

It's dead quiet. Instinctively, she glances at the clock on the dashboard: it glows 12:53. But she never bothers to adjust for daylight savings time, so automatically subtracts an hour. Nearly midnight. Too late to knock on Jack's door. He's been asleep for hours, has a date at dawn with the mewling trapline. She doesn't want to wake him, to admit she has been foolhardy enough to come out in this storm. To answer his predictable questions: Why didn't you stay in the city? Why were you out in the first place?

An advanced SLR photography class. At least that's what she told her husband. But the class would have ended hours ago, nine at the latest. If it existed. It does exist—she carefully checked the curriculum details in the college calendar—but not for her. She isn't enrolled. Such classes hold scant interest for her, though she once gobbled them greedily like the screaming blue jays that bolt and scatter sunflower seeds at the kitchen door feeder. She's sated now, prefers to work in the darkroom she has set up in the washroom at the back of her shop, the washroom being for staff use only and she being the sole staff and owner. It's convenient to work there during the joyously long lulls between customers. And it's a new building, so is less dusty than home, the old farmhouse. It's easier to keep the negatives pristine.

Pristine. There's an apt word. Like the snow, like she tries to keep her life. Compartmentalized, simple. Of course, it's utterly unsustainable. The negative will attract dust, the snow will turn mushy and grey, her life will get messy. Especially the way that she lives it: moving madly about, point A to point B, not pausing for a moment to consider.

I wonder if Stefan sees me as someone striving for a pristine life, devoid of gummy human emotions? Is that why he gave me this book? Sneaky. Well, he'd be wrong. I've earned a quiet life. Besides I have friends, I just don't need to see them very often.

There is no class. But if there were, thinking of it from Jack's view, she would have come home promptly, when the storm began, instead of waiting, going for a glass of wine with her classmates.

If she had been there. But she hadn't.

There is no way of explaining anything simply to the neighbour, she decides. She will look a fool, or worse, a liar. Better to get home, to slip into bed beside her husband who will snore lightly and shift under the down duvet.

All things considered there is only one option: walk home. Past the next neighbour's house, then perhaps another kilometre, to their house at the dead end. Or is it a bit farther?

Oh, big surprise! Of course she's stuck. How I loathe predictable stories. If I wanted predictable, I'd stop reading altogether and just look out the window. And she's behaving like a child. Why not go to Jack's, for Chrissakes! This ruse about the class —Jack wouldn't question that. But she's so scared of getting caught in her lies that she isn't thinking rationally. Typical. It's not the lying that gets people into trouble—it's their anxiety about it. And the more complicated the lies, the greater the probability of getting caught.

Stefan's lie is multi-layered. You might think it's not a lie, but it is: lying by
omission. Neglecting to say what's really on his mind. This flurry of visits all of a
sudden — it's not my charming conversational skills drawing him in — and the
questions about what I had for dinner. Pretending he doesn't know the name of the
PM. He's trying to figure out if I'm tumbling down the slippery slope of dementia.
Why doesn't he just say so?

    At least her lies are simple. The problem is she's afraid of what might happen if
her lies are exposed. If? Actually, when. Because that's the other thing: the longer
she lies, the more likely she is to be found out. So here she sits. Stuck. The car cool-
ing and clicking as she hedges her bets.

She remembers the first time she came to her husband's house — how she loved its seclusion. It seemed to be hiding around that final turn in the road. It reminded her of how Frank Lloyd Wright hid the entrances to his buildings behind a hedge or a half wall, affording residents an extra measure of privacy, a separation from the outside world. She found the idea of seclusion, of being hidden, attractive. She could work without distraction, almost in a void. No shops within walking distance, no yoga class to attend. No casual visitors or neighbours seeking a cup of sugar. Alone. Oh, but with him there, too. Of course. Here she could sort her negatives, shape her exhibits. Not pretty pictures. God, no. She's had three exhibits now at a prominent art gallery in the city. All concern the flotsam and jetsam of our society: a valued possession, with inherent meaning, contrasted with abandoned objects that once held meaning in the context of ownership and all that entails:

An old-fashioned, blond-haired doll, years old, still in its packaging.
A broken doll, one blinking eye missing, the other askew, its body tracked with scribbles of magic markers.
A cabinet filled with carefully arranged, rarely used Royal Doulton china, a piece of carefully cut tissue between the plates lest they scrape one another.
A chipped Limoges teacup, stained with rings from countless abandoned cups of orange pekoe tea.

The former, the valued objects, she gleans through conversations with her customers, who are pleased to have their treasures photographed. The latter she mostly finds at her local dump, where she brings the trash and recyclables on alternate Thursday mornings. She has befriended the caretaker, has gotten used to the port-wine stain that covers most of his face. He saves things for her now. Often off the mark, but she photographs them anyway because she wants to encourage him. Her new exhibit will focus on the dump alone—the things we give away, abandon. The fleeting stuff of our lives, the stuff we once thought brought meaning to who we are.

At least that was the idea, a year ago, but now she finds it lifeless, which of course it is. But she is unable to get on with it, or to shed this project altogether and move on. The gallery owner keeps phoning, asking when he can schedule her next show. She is noncommittal. She considers whether she might be depressed, might regain her momentum by taking a pill, a low dose to tweak her mood but leave her creativity intact. It might even make her kinder to her husband, more accommodating in the night, more tolerant of his long silences, his preoccupation with his books, his consumption of them.

He is the consumer, she has decided. She is the producer. Perhaps that was their initial attraction. But gradually, she came to know by the way he gobbled books, that he lacked appreciation. A glutton, not a gourmand after all. This was bolstered by the fact that he never discussed what he had read, other than to pronounce that he had finished X or Y—as if it were an item on the menu—and had moved on to the next course, Z.

Of course she's depressed. Not depressed, take-an-SSRI depressed, but old-fashioned down in the dumps. And who wouldn't be? Stuck in the middle of nowhere with a robo-husband who shows no interest in her. I understand her need to isolate herself so she can create art, but she's taken it too far. I'm isolated too, but unlike her, I'm content. Why can't she take the leap and leave? And if she can't dredge up the confidence, why wouldn't she look for help from her friends? Does she have any? Maybe she's succumbed to the modern fallacy that a marriage, a so-called good marriage, should fulfill all our needs for love, intimacy, friendship. What a Cinderella happily-ever-after crock. Her husband has found company in his books. Like me. Though I, at least, don't dine and dash. I consider what I've read, try to make some sense of it.

Earlier, before they married, he offered intelligent remarks about her first solo show, *The Things We Hold Dear*. He spoke of the inevitable disappointment of consumerism, of the conceit of ownership. He seemed interested in art—certainly he knew the language. They had met at an exhibit of photos depicting the Second World War, the exhibit where she saw the Eisenstaedt photo of the sailor kissing the nurse. They discussed the exhibit afterward over a cup of coffee. He knew so much about history, politics, war. And he seemed interested in her. He was promising. She mistakenly thought he was the sort of man who enjoyed discussing ideas. But, gradually, over the ensuing years, the conversation dwindled. Perhaps he had nothing new to say. He is a man who does not repeat himself. Perhaps he is not moved by her new works, and so says nothing. She doesn't know and hasn't asked. Gradually, almost imperceptibly, he spoke less and less. He lost articles, then adjectives, adverbs. Soon, all that will be left are nouns and verbs: 'Shopping. Saturday. Lasagna?' This is the inevitable future.

What a drama queen! As if anyone could be that poor at communicating. He's probably fed up with her antics. She has that artistic temperament, real or manu-factured. If only she'd calm down and try to understand the situation, try to really talk to him instead of waiting for him to show interest in her. I feel for the guy. It's all about her and her next destination. Then again, you could say the same for most people. Always so intent on moving to point B, there's no opportunity for reflec-tion, for finding their way.

Easy for me to say, you might think, I'm retired. But it isn't a matter of time—it's attitude. Take Stefan. He's a busy guy but he knows what's up, he recognizes his foibles. Of course, he thinks he knows mine too, which is annoying.

That's why he gave me this book. I'm sure of it. Who gives therapy to the therapist?

She shivers in the cooling car and considers her clothes: high boots of thin leather with a two-inch heel. Not made for trudging through snow on country lanes, but at least tall enough to keep the snow out. She hopes. Her faux-fur coat comes nearly to her knees and is warm. Vintage, so the sleeves are a bit short because subsequent generations have grown taller. Her green leather gloves are unlined, intended for driving and fashion, but her coat pockets are deep, deep enough to hold her hands and wrists—or most of them. She curses herself for wearing a skirt—short as he, her lover, likes it—but at least with tights. Thankfully, she pulled a pair of ankle socks over her feet. And her hat, her trademark black wool beret. Perched askance, rakishly, in the city, but it can be pulled down, mostly covering her ears, and nestled in the coat collar.... Oh, and the scarf. It's purple pashmina. And fake, no doubt made of acrylic, but long and wide, shawl-like. She pulls it over her dark hair, wraps it around her neck, pulls the beret on top, buttons the coat all the way up. Slings her compact red purse over her head, across her chest. She is ready.

High-heeled boots! She's like Eva whatshername in Green Acres—*a sitcom cliché. And the lover ... she would resort to a physical connection. A hormone buzz is so much simpler than anything real. What doesn't fit here is the husband. How can he be so blind? And if he does know, wouldn't he leave her? Or is he indifferent as she says? That's worse than jealousy. Indifference: the opposite of love.*

I should know. Thirty-two years of marriage and Phillip walked. Said he didn't love me anymore. Truth is he didn't even like me. He was indifferent. Well, his loss, because now he's in a cheesy old-folks' home, two to a room, motivational posters on the walls, calorie-counted meals. Alone.

Maybe that's what this woman's husband fears—being alone. But she isn't logical. If he's as indifferent as she believes, he wouldn't care about her love affair, so why bother hiding it? I open the book, search for my place:

All things considered ...

No, farther along than that ...

She opens the car door, pushes first gently, then more firmly against the drift of snow. It is deep, but light. Filled with air. A cold January snow, not laden with moisture as it will be in the months to come. She steps out. It's not as deep as she feared, comes to a few inches below the top of her boot.

She wonders if she should have stayed in the city. Feigned a sleepover with a girlfriend or a classmate. But who? And what details could she fabricate, because she would be with him, naturally. Except for the need for those details, it would have been easy to stay in his cozy bed under the fibre-filled duvet. He is allergic to down, to feathers in general.

It's so dark—moon, stars, sky, all gone. All she sees is the snow in front of her face. Lately, the frisson, the thrill of getting away with something, is absent. She feels disquiet, is no longer quite sure that her affairs do no harm. She shakes away her anxiety. Get moving, she thinks.

To divert herself, she plays her usual game: making up pictures. Two images juxtaposed:

A candle melted and stuck into a dark blue, chipped-glass holder, the dish of which is caked in muted colours of melted wax. Stuck in it is a carelessly closed sticky bottle of massage oil.

A tall, white tapered candle towers in its crystal holder, which rests on an invitation in linen stationery. A wedding invitation it seems, judging by the font and gold emboss.

She shakes her head. Cliché, she thinks. She peers down the road. The way should be easy to find, the road cuts a swath through the dark forest. Follow it and I will get there, she reassures herself, but notices the snow has already coated the shoulders of her faux-fur.

If she's careful, she should be able to keep the snow out of her boots.

She shuffles forward; there's no point in trying to lift her feet over the deep snow. She makes her way to the front of the car, tracing her finger through the white coating its sides. By morning, the car will be invisible, consumed by nature. It happens so quickly, she thinks. If she neglects weeding the midsummer garden even for a couple of weeks, nature infiltrates, crown vetch blooms suddenly, its rampant runners taking hours to unearth, to stop the invasion.

She sets out, down the hill that would have been so easy in the car. The wind picks up, blows behind her. Snow swirls around her body. At least I'm not leaning into the wind, she thinks. A bit of good luck. No, luck has nothing to do with it, she corrects herself. She made this situation.

She believes people who have affairs are only caught if they aren't careful. She believes that, subconsciously, they want to be caught. She is conscious, methodical. She keeps the lies simple and as few as possible so they are easy to remember, to retell, to reanimate. She creates a finite alternate universe. A class in the city: darkroom techniques. That's easy to feign. Besides, she knows her husband will never ask about it. She, in turn, has adopted his habitual reticence and never volunteers anything. It's best that way. Safe and simple.

She hears the trees, the rustle of leaves on the oak, leftover from the fertile summer, now dead and dry, clinging to slender twigs.

A branch creaks. Is that a moan? It sounds human, she thinks, but knows it's the frozen trees convulsing in the malicious wind.

Her cheeks are already numb and there is a bracelet of skin at the top of her wrists, above her gloves, that is icy cold. She jams her hands deeper into her pockets, but her wrists are still partially exposed. There's nothing I can do, she thinks. It will have to be endured. The snow is deeper now, over her boots. The fabric of her tights is wet, clinging to her kneecaps and that tender place behind.

She reaches the bottom of the hill where the forest briefly clears on either side, permitting the stream to cut a path, then traverse the road through the culvert that overflows in spring. It's not so far to the Cookes' house now, she thinks, though she has never walked the road in winter—certainly never in a storm.

She begins to climb the hill where the forest is at its thickest. She hears a shuffling in the woods, in the undergrowth, then, in the distance, a yip. Perhaps a wild dog. Another sound. Then a howl. She shivers. He's far away, she thinks. We hear them all the time, nothing to worry about. Keep moving. Up the hill.

Wild dogs? They'll be hungry in the middle of winter. Even she's scared, I can see that, yet she ignores her instincts. Why not head back to Jack's? She's a fool for getting into this situation in the first place and a fool now for not doing the smart thing, the safe thing. That's how most people land in trouble. Trudging on, hoping danger will pass them by. Some would call it bravery, or courage. But courage is not the absence of fear—it's the overwhelming feeling that something else is more important than fear. In this case, her need for secrecy. Is she afraid that if her husband discovers her secret life she might actually have to do something about her marriage? Is she afraid of living honestly?

Stefan says that's how people see me: someone who lives in secrecy, unengaged. He's such a know-it-all. I am engaged. I keep up with the news.

She pushes upward, up the long hill toward the pasture where Mr Cooke keeps the sheep so he can watch them from the house when they are close to lambing. Other times he pastures them farther afield, kept watch by a giant Komondor dog draped in dirty-white dreadlocks. He's trained to guard livestock, spends all his time alone in remote fields that are half-infiltrated by the pervasive junipers. She's afraid of the dog, of meeting him on the road or in a field.

She thinks she should have stayed in the city, imagines him, her lover, nestled in his bed. He wanted her to stay, urged her to stay when the storm picked up. She could have told her husband that she had gone to a motel. Somewhere cheap. Yes, that's what she could have said. Why was she in such a rush to get home? It's not as if he would miss me, she thinks.

She could have stayed, phoned early in the morning to say she couldn't risk the weather. *It's my guilt that propelled me out in this.*

She trudges through the snow. Guilt, yes. That and her reluctance to stay over, she admits. She didn't want to. It would be too intimate—more even than sex—seeing each other naked in the morning without the benefit of wine and dim lighting. She doesn't want that.

Still, she could have actually gone to a motel. By the time she phoned in the morning, he would have been busy getting ready for work, which mostly involves nibbling toast with sticky jam while reading one of his interminable World War II history books—his major interest at university, though he never finished the degree—then pulling on his faded blue overalls moments before driving away.

His shift at the printing plant is seven to three; her shop is open ten to six, Tuesdays through Saturdays. Sunday is their only day off together. Neither complains about this. Their life is calm. The chores are divided evenly. He cooks the evening meals and does the shopping. She keeps the house clean enough, struggles with the garden and lawn, takes the trash to the dump. He tends to the firewood and arranges for the ploughman and repairs. They've tamed the drudgery of the day-to-day, the things her girlfriends complain about—or used to when she still bothered to keep in touch, before she was married and moved out here. It's not so far from the city—only an hour in good weather—but far enough to deter casual visits for a coffee or lunch. It's a quiet life, but she can always escape to the city when the need arises.

Why bother going to the hassle of living with someone if there's no connection, no intimacy? They're like roommates. She'd be better off alone. But she's too afraid. I think she's afraid of intimacy with herself. And instead, what does she get? A feeble marriage and sex with some guy in the city? She drives a hundred kilometres for an orgasm. A bit of physical contact. Sex disguised as love. Why doesn't she just take matters into her own hands? Guaranteed pleasure, that. And you can order the gizmos online too. Maybe she'll learn. Maybe this trip through the snow will wake her up. I do think she's an appealing character. She tries so hard. And I like her art, or at least the way it's described. But it's no wonder she's stuck there, too. No wonder when her life is so contained.

She takes stock. Her feet, despite the extra socks, are cold in the thin leather boots, but more or less dry. Dryish. Her wrists are numb now, but even worse is the skin at the top of the boots; the fabric of her tights is frozen, as is the skin below. Thank goodness the boot top is elasticized so the snow hasn't crept down under the leather. Not yet anyway.

Her eyes catch a flash of something in the forest to her right. My imagination? she wonders fearfully. She stops, turns to stare, sees nothing beyond the snow. Then there! Another glitter. Two. Eyes? An animal? A fox? A wild dog? Her husband told her that they were afraid of people, wouldn't meddle, that she shouldn't be afraid. He said this kindly, didn't make fun of her city-slicker ways. Despite this reassurance, her heart pounds. She feels her body heat rising. Her intellectual knowing is suddenly at cross-purposes with her emotional feeling. The flash does not come back. It's gone. My imagination, she thinks. Those eyes. What light are they reflecting anyway? There's nothing out here. 'Hey,' she calls out. The sound deadens immediately, consumed by snow. 'Hey!'

She keeps moving. The ground levels out, the forest ends abruptly. She has reached the pasture. Suddenly the snow is much deeper; it has blown across the pasture, accumulated on the road. It's well over her knee, up to mid-thigh. Still it is light, not damp. If I keep brushing it off it won't melt, she thinks.

She tries to increase her pace, but it's difficult pushing through the drifts. The wind has picked up, too, and switched around to blow against her. The icy snow bites at her face. She pulls the scarf up over her chin and mouth, pulls it down to cover her forehead.

She thinks of her lover, stroking her cheeks, her forehead, telling her she is beautiful—the lover's mantra. She knows it's not entirely true. Her nose is crooked, her eyes too small. But she does have a charm. And she dresses like an artist: a mélange of vintage and contemporary, with chunky jewellery and always a hat. A clashing style that he appreciates, though it mystifies people in the town. He says he loves her. She says nothing, just smiles. He is not like previous lovers, the ones she had to leave, the ones who would have eventually urged her to leave her husband.

He doesn't want to know about the husband. Says he finds it difficult to think of her cheating, feels guilty enough toward this unknown man. Knowing about him would be too difficult; he would become real, a person with feelings and thoughts. No, no, no, he doesn't want to know. That's best for her too. Easier. She likes him for this. He's not the most skilled lover she's ever had, but he's certainly the least demanding. She can enter his world fresh, uncontaminated by a past. He does not love me, she realizes, despite what he says. He's a sexual partner and that's all he can ever be. This realization is new to her. She tests it like bathwater, finds it a bit cold. If this is true, is it worth the lies? Is it worth this?

Is she finally waking to reality? To the shallowness of her quest for an orgasm? To the fact you can't get everything you need—best friend, colleague, partner, lover—from one person? No wonder she finds her husband so lacking, why she's terminally dissatisfied. And the price? Now even she's starting to realize it's too high. Comes of having to slow down for a minute or two. You can't figure anything out if you're always rushing to the next thing. It's getting late.

I wonder where Stefan is? Traffic maybe. He'll come, he's a reliable sort. And he leaves on holiday tomorrow, so I won't see him for two weeks. I hate to admit it, but I'm going to miss him.

The snow changes suddenly to pellets: sharp teeth that sting as they strike her cheeks. She pulls the scarf more closely around her face, adjusts her faux-fur collar. Up ahead, she sees the streetlight that marks a sharp turn in the road. It's odd to have such a light in the middle of the country, but the Cookes are odd men.

The son does most of the farming. He never married, lives in a falling-down farmhouse with his elderly father. The mother—the wife—is long dead, probably of neglect and overwork. One of the outbuildings is filled with beer bottles. She wonders why they don't return them for the deposit.

They could probably use the money. Is it shame? Did they accumulate gradually, and now it's too late to do anything about it? Is it easier to leave things as they are, pretend the inevitable will not happen, that the cabin will never fill completely? She's met the younger Mr Cooke a half-dozen times along the road. Last time was in late fall and he asked if she'd heard any wild dogs. Coyotes, he called them. Of course she had heard the howls, no closer than usual though.

'No closer,' she says aloud now.

He told her the coyotes were after the sheep, had 'eaten the hind-quarters off one of 'em'. At the time, she'd asked him why his Komondor didn't scare off the coyotes. He said the dog was no fuckin' good. Half-wild herself and expensive to feed. He was thinking of getting rid of her.

A practical fellow. Unsentimental.

She shivers, not only with cold, and an image enters her head:

A trap holds the leg of an ermine, its white fur artfully flecked with blood, except at its leg, which is raw with blood and flesh where the trap's teeth are clamped and it has attempted to gnaw free. A Ski-Doo boot protrudes into the upper right corner of the photo. The ermine's head dangles to the lower left.

But her images always come in twos, and so another:

Close-up on a wild dog's bright eyes, brown muzzle and teeth, which grip a human hand, a woman's hand with blood drizzling over a diamond solitaire engagement ring, running over a slightly chipped French manicure, dripping and disappearing into the spongy, decaying leaves that cover the ground.

No, she thinks, shaking her head, that's not helpful. She concentrates on her steps. The streetlight gleams through the falling snow like a light-house, welcoming and warning as she passes under it. The dark bulk of the Cookes' house looms in the distance. She tries to walk faster—it would be creepy to encounter either of the Cooke men at night. She trudges up a slight rise curving to the right. The snow is less deep now, but has seeped beneath the elastic at the top of her boot. The fabric is frozen; her leg beneath is numb. Her feet feel heavy, leaden. She stumbles then rights herself.

Their house isn't far now. She's come more than halfway. A couple of rises and falls in the road, a turn left, then right—the streetlight disappears as she follows the road.

She sees something lying across the road. A body? No, a tree. She squints. Yes. Yes, down in the storm. At the top of the rise, where the trees line the road. Behind them, half-open pastures are plagued with wild junipers. It's one of the old maples, she realizes. I'll miss the red leaves come fall. The flash of brilliance. The tree is only lightly covered in a sifting of snow. When did it come down? she wonders. Ten minutes ago? Less than an hour? No, not even that long. There would be more snow cover. It could have come down on me, if I hadn't stayed those extra few minutes, lingering in bed. If I had left when I had originally thought I should . . . then, this. She pushes the idea away.

What? Our nameless heroine is still in denial? I thought she was waking up. Seems she's a committed sleepwalker. Doesn't she understand that another tree could come crashing down, could crush or pin her with no one to hear her calls? See why I don't go out? Of course, the burbs aren't fraught like the countryside—that's an order of magnitude more hazardous.

Stefan says he'll take me to the mall this afternoon. He'll drive slowly, he says, and we'll only stay fifteen minutes, a half-hour tops. He treats me like I'm some doddering idiot. I don't see why I should go, there's nothing I need and malls are not entertaining for me, but if it makes him happy. . . . Am I afraid? Of what exactly? Consuming-crazy fools and bad drivers? Maybe our heroine is clever to push her fear out of her mind so she can keep going, do what needs to be done. Maybe I should take a page out of her book. This book. Ha!

The wind picks up, roars across the field. Pellets of snow bombard her face. She can scarcely keep her eyes open. Her feet are ice blocks. She plods along, hunkers down into her coat, feels she is smaller than she was before. Almost there, she thinks, almost, but the thought fails to lift her spirits. She pictures her husband, lying in wait in their cramped double bed. Despite his daytime reticence, his silences and truncated speech, he seeks her out under covers. She shivers. He is a selfish lover. His own needs foremost, supplanting foreplay or forethought. There is scant kissing—he doesn't like tongues touching, is repelled by the idea of sharing fluids, germs. Doesn't like fellatio either, which was fine by her initially, but then she discovered, with a lover, the joy in giving intense pleasure. She wonders why her husband, who is self-absorbed in his pleasure seeking, is so against it. It must be the repugnant idea of reciprocity.

A question comes into her head: Why do I stay? She has not asked herself this for a long time, years. Way back she decided it was too soon to give up, that with time, they'd find a life together. This is where time has led me, she thinks, down a trail of lies, so she scarcely knows what is real. Lies she thought freed her, allowed her to live calmly, making her art. She grimaces; her half-frozen face hurts with the movement. Now she doesn't even have the art. She thinks of lying with him, lying to him in that bed with its towering head- and footboards. A relic from the nineteenth century, not even quite a double. That bed of his forebears: his parents, grandparents, all had lain there before them in matrimony. All the people, pain, pathos. Joy, loving, promises. All these ghosts in that bed they now share like roommates. The word solidifies for her, takes form. That is what we are: roommates. There is no love on either side of the bed. There is familiarity, born of knowing each other a long time, an ability to get along. And there's convenience. But we are separate. Him: his books. Me: the photos. And my secrets. He knows, she suddenly realizes. Of course he knows. He's probably known for years. It doesn't matter to him. So who exactly have I been cheating?

Now she's coming to some real understanding. Her instincts are right, her husband does know. He probably sees it as the price he has to pay, given the sort of man he is: content with his own company, reticent. He accepts that he can't give her everything she needs. And she believes she's found solace in others. But now that she understands the narrowness of the contract, can she continue? It is a question I settled for myself long ago, propelled by Phillip, of course, but still. . . . We have to make our peace or be consumed by the quest.

She starts up the hill toward the driveway. Stands of trees close in on the road again. The snow has nearly stopped, but she can't see the light from the porch. Normally, they leave it on for each other out of habit, a courtesy. She seeks the light. I will sleep in the spare room tonight, she vows. I will move in there tomorrow. If the road is clear, I will go into town and buy a new single bed. An art piece pops into her mind:

Their double bed, with the quilt covering a pile of people, all his ancestors, a leg and arm sticking out here and there.
An empty single bed, the plain coverlet pulled taut over a single female form, tucked in tightly.

There is still no porch light. I should be there by now, she says aloud, hearing the panic in her voice. I should be there, she thinks. She hears a noise, a padding of feet and turns to look behind her. The road she has just come up seems unfamiliar. She squints, struggling to see her footprints, but they seem to have vanished. Did she come that way, or did she somehow get turned around? She turns again, sees footprints, large, canine. A dog? A wild dog? She jerks to the left. Her scarf falls down and icy wind batters her face. She feels its approach for a second, then it is there: a swish of an animal—large and dirty-white—knocks her down. She falls into the snow.

It's as I feared. The giant dog from next door, something half-domestic being scarier than something wholly wild. It's her own fault, but I feel sorry for her, just when she was getting somewhere.

There's the bell. Stefan.

PART TWO

Dispatches from Madawan

BITTER
BUTTER

Betty Botter bought some butter. Or so the tongue twister goes. In reality, she bought more than some. She bought three pounds and she longed to buy more. She also bought two pints of heavy cream, some for the lentil soup and butter chicken, the rest for the crème brûlée. Yes, it was a heavy meal, but that was the norm in the Butter Club, as she'd dubbed the weekly dinners that brought together four couples, all neighbours in Madawan.

'Friendship by proximity,' she joked with her closest neighbour, Tammy Tucker. Proximity did play a part. It permitted frequent evening visits among the women, ostensibly to borrow a cup of this or that, but actually to escape, if only for twenty minutes, the hubbub of their households after a demanding day at work and a tedious commute. The women had married quickly, just as their final viable eggs were ripening. They knew their men were fixer-uppers when they married them; the women were all professionally successful but failures in this domestic task.

Food was the binding ingredient of their friendship, and it dominated their conversation. 'Foodies' was too frivolous a moniker to describe their devotion, their search for the freshest, the best, the most hormone-and-antibiotic free. Their shopping was state of the art, involving baskets of seasonal produce delivered to their homes and out-of-the-way drives to source ethically raised, humanely killed meat—all according to the latest trends. But their cooking was the antithesis of trendy. Homemade baking soda biscuits served with creamy cheeses, deep red paprika chicken and savoury goulash, chocolate raspberry cheesecake and deep-dish pecan pie—all had fallen out of favour amidst peer-reviewed studies about swelling obesity rates. On Saturdays, the women cooked all day, but ate relatively little; the men polished their plates with homemade white bread.

The descent into this calorific state of affairs was gradual, insidious. Or so it seemed. A rich dessert now and again became the norm. Then the biscuit-and-cheese course was introduced, and was much clamoured for by the husbands. Then Betty Botter tried some French cuisine and the other wives followed suit. Their Saturday feasts were anticipated all week but, unbeknownst to one another, they had allowed this cuisine to spill over into every day. Even packed-lunch sandwiches were primed with mayonnaise on generously proportioned buttered bread, then topped with cheese and slabs of ham. There were no complaints from their husbands. The children, of course, got healthier fare, lest the school monitors raise an alarm. Betty Botter noted with satisfaction her husband's emerging double chin.

Gradually an idea began simmering in each of the women's heads—an idea that they likewise kept to themselves. Each had been long married and long dissatisfied. Each had long ago given up on therapy or the hope that their dull husbands might actually prove to become the sort of men they'd hoped to fashion. Divorce was out of the question given bulky mortgages and small children, the expectations of parents and the spectre of public failure.

Betty Botter whipped her butter to a creamy froth before gently folding in the flour and a dash of vanilla. Her famous butter cookies, to be served with the crème brûlée that night, topped with raspberry preserve. Overkill.

Everyone said that dinner was her best ever. The men were too full to waddle down to the basement for their habitual game of billiards. Betty Botter noted that two of them seemed to have gained weight in the week since the last Butter Club. Wishful thinking, she admonished herself. She served coffee, liberally laced with Baileys Irish Cream. As she handed a cup to Tammy Tucker, their eyes met. Tammy Tucker smiled and murmured, 'Five pounds.'

Betty Botter smiled back and quickly served the others, but Tammy Tucker's words stuck in her mind. What did she mean? She eyed her closely, she didn't seem to have gained weight, but her husband was another matter. He was swelling, it seemed to Betty Botter. Over dishes in the kitchen, she whispered to her friend, 'This week?'

Tammy Tucker nodded. 'And yours?' she asked.

'He won't go on a scale; I'd guess two a week.'

The third neighbour, Roberta Rutter, came in with the empty ramekins. 'Mine's up twenty since Christmas,' she said.

The women looked at one another without blinking, none able to put her deepest desires into words.

Roberta Rutter's husband was the first to go: congestive heart failure. 'Family history,' she intoned from beneath her fetching black veil. Betty Botter wondered, but didn't say anything. Patricia Pundit winked at her as she put out cutlery. They had all pitched in to prepare the funeral feast. Their signature sandwiches, slathered with mayonnaise, cream cheese and butter, were prudently replaced with lighter fillings. Appearances had to be kept up.

Betty Botter's husband held out the longest; the children were in their early teens. For the funeral feast she borrowed Roberta Rutter's veil and hid her dry eyes. She devoured a barely dressed salad, smacking her lips with pleasure.

BEST
BEFORE

I judge people by the groceries they bring through my checkout. I know this isn't fair—they could be buying for their physically challenged aunt or their alcohol-abusing neighbour—but I do it anyway. It gives me something interesting to think about at work. My favourite customers are the pasty-faced anemic couple who come through every Thursday evening, buggy brimming with Fritos, Diet Coke, boil-in-a-bag entrees and microwaveable TV dinners. Nothing fresh. Nothing green.

I have this theory. I measure how sexually satisfied people are by the amount of junk food they buy. The more junk, the more the need for oral gratification, intense munching in front of the television. My anemic couple is obviously having sexual difficulties.

I've been coming home with huge bags of Doritos myself these days.

My wife comes to bed with pointed metal clips in her permed hair to keep it buoyant—metal life preservers for her sinking coiffure. I kiss her carefully to avoid getting impaled on these instruments of beauty. Her cheek is slightly greasy with moisturizer. She is trying to preserve her skin. I read the packages: 'Unique moisture complex helps smooth away wrinkle lines. Enhances skin hydration through efficient water delivery system.' I imagine her bloated, completely hydrated without any lines at all, just a smooth oval with perfectly coiffed hair on top.

I'm the assistant manager at Jim's FOOD on the corner of Willow and First in downtown Madawan. Jim is huge—a lunar eclipse of a man. He is always pinching my upper arm, urging me to try the FOOD pasta line. 'You're not much of an endorsement,' he says in his PA-system voice, loudly guffawing afterwards, making me wonder when I can retire. I stand at my cash register, mind immobile, fingers moving:

Jamaican bell peppers—vegetable code 69—$1.33

Chicken noodle soup (special)—89¢

The Ultimate Tampons (a unique FOOD product)—$4.29

During quiet moments I sometimes read the ingredients on the packages. My favourite part is the 'May contain' list. I make up my own: Life may contain unusual amounts of general malaise sodium glutamate. Relationships may contain dehydrogenated unhappiness. I marvel at how little I know about the science of the food industry.

My wife's shoulder pads are getting bigger. They used to be scant, barely accentuating her natural curves. Now she sticks thick foam pads directly onto her bare shoulders. Sweaty foam against her smooth skin. 'In-Shape' they're called. 'Enhances your wardrobe and flatters your figure.' She looks like a quarterback. She's calling a passing game but never follows her own signals. I don't know what will happen next.

Her shoulder pads are gigantic now—offensive tackle size. Soon she'll have to turn sideways to pass through the bedroom doorway.

I'm bruising the produce. I caught myself gripping grapefruits the other day, one in each hand, squeezing gently. I glanced furtively at the customer who was mercifully diving into the bottom of her cart to retrieve a bag of Oreos. I quickly keyed in 'Grapefruit, 2 @ 99¢'—and grabbed the porterhouse steaks.

Today my anemic couple bought a bunch of bananas. This depresses me beyond measure.

My wife has started using strange beauty products. She squeezes her eyelashes with metal tongs to curl them. It looks like she's plucking her eyeballs out. She's bought Jolen to bleach the shadowy hairs on her upper lip. I liked their scant darkness, the way drops of sweat would bead there when we made love. Now they are pale, almost invisible, totally innocuous.

Sometimes she uses an apricot facial mask. 'Deep-cleanses pores and gives skin a luminous sheen.' Her eyes peer out of the stark white as she files her nails and watches *Sex and the City* reruns. She can't laugh—the mask is too tight—so she chortles and snorts.

I read: 'Kool-Aid may contain tricalcium phosphate.' Millions of kids are gulping water softener. I glance up from the cash register and am surprised to see my wife coming into the store. She never does the grocery shopping, food is *my* business. I peer around my cash register and see her shoulders sway down the cleaning goods/toiletries aisle. The muzak seems louder; I have to ask Mr Leeuwen to repeat what he's said.

'I have a coupon for the Premium Plus,' he bellows.

I forget to charge for three tins of Friskies cat food. I don't care.

Then she's standing at my cash. She's started to wear a dark shade of lipstick—'Raspberry Stain' it's called. I have covertly watched her face in the mirror as she applies it, carefully outlining her mouth with a matching pencil, using a small brush to apply the lipstick in controlled strokes. She is impossible to get near now. I fear her huge, red, indelible smudges.

I say hello or something, smile grudgingly. She's buying an over-sized bag of FOOD cotton balls and two yellowish-red mangoes. I put them in a plastic FOOD bag. The mangoes are surprisingly heavy, ripe. I can't believe she's buying fresh fruit. I avoid her eyes, fearful I might betray my suspicion. My theory. I take the money and give her change.

'See you later,' I mutter as I turn to the next customer.

At supper that night I watch her mouth as she eats. She doesn't swallow one mouthful before inserting the next. I glimpse her molars mashing pork chop with green beans with potatoes. She takes her plate to the sink and returns with one of the mangoes and a sharp paring knife. She carefully removes all the peel, then bites in. Juice oozes out of the corners of her mouth and dribbles down her chin. She doesn't offer me any.

DISPATCHES FROM MADAWAN

I left my husband three years ago and took the manual typewriter. It's a tiny Underwood portable for travelling correspondents—war correspondents. Instead of the usual forty-one keys, it has twenty-six. The shift is for punctuation marks and numbers. There are no lower case letters; text is UPPER CASE ONLY. I keep the typewriter in case of nuclear attack.

It's not like I'm paranoid. I don't have an air raid shelter lined with shelves of canned or dehydrated food, or a gun, or anything like that. But it's comforting to know that I have the typewriter, something to communicate with, to leave messages and warnings for survivors. It seems hopeful, given the scenario.

I didn't use to think this way, but after my son was born I began having nuclear holocaust nightmares.

I LOAD THE CAR WITH ESSENTIALS: SLEEPING BAGS, FOOD, TOOLS, SEEDS FOR HARDY CABBAGES AND CARROTS, WARM CLOTHES. THEN MY SON AND I HEAD NORTH TO OUTRUN THE EFFECTS OF DEVASTATION. MY HUSBAND IS LEFT BEHIND WITH THE PHOTO ALBUMS AND ELECTRICAL APPLIANCES, OF NO VALUE IN A SURVIVAL SITUATION.

The typewriter sits on the basement floor, but I'm thinking of moving it to a spot on the new bookshelf. A stack of notebooks and papers sits there now—five inches of details about another mother's nightmare. About a son murdered in Thailand. Allegedly. It's difficult to know the truth. His mother, my source, keeps enticing me into her version of the story, making me believe that she must be right.

The authorities say her nineteen-year-old son committed suicide while vacationing in Thailand two months ago. Joyce says he was murdered. She carries around a plastic Madawan FOOD shopping bag filled with rumpled, coffee-stained papers explaining to anyone who will listen that she has evidence: found documents, time differences in the official records of events, tales of reluctant, nervous officials, faded photocopies. She is convinced that her son did not jump off the roof of the Bangkok Police Station. ('The police station, for Christ's sake,' she says. 'What was he doing there?')

My editor at the *Ottawa Star* says it could develop into a great story—a massive cover-up or a legendary tale of bureaucratic bungling. So I keep listening to Joyce and, occasionally, writing updates.

MADAWAN, ONT.—A LOCAL WOMAN WANTS THE RCMP TO LAUNCH AN INVESTIGATION INTO THE DEATH OF HER SON IN BANGKOK, THAILAND. ACCORDING TO JOYCE RICHTER, THAI AUTHORITIES CLAIM HER SON, 19-YEAR-OLD STEVE RICHTER, COMMITTED SUICIDE.

She's gone through External Affairs, CSIS, the RCMP and now she's on to the local OPP, trying to convince them that they can launch an international investigation through some loophole in law enforcement regulations. Joyce talks about it all the time. Now she cries on the phone while she's talking to me. I don't know whether she's right and is using everything she has—facts and emotions—to convince me, or if she simply can't accept that her son committed suicide. Either way I sympathize with her. She lost her son.

My nephew was two when he drowned in three inches of green rainwater in the bottom of a cracked goldfish pond. My brother said he was there with his wife, and he, too, turned his back for that moment when the little fellow slipped out through the patio doors.

MADAWAN, ONT.—TWO-AND-A-HALF-YEAR-OLD NATHAN WRIGHT
DROWNED IN A FISH POND BEHIND A YONGE ST. RESIDENCE YESTER-
DAY. HIS PARENTS, NATALIE AND ROBERT WRIGHT, WERE UNAVAILABLE
FOR COMMENT.

I remember the metre-long white coffin buried in white roses and baby's breath. Our relatives came in from across the country—I'd never seen so many of them, not even for weddings. Years later, long after my son was born, I learned that my sister-in-law was alone when it happened. My brother lied to protect her, to take equal responsibility. 'It could have happened to anyone,' he told me. I've read that ninety-five per cent of marriages break up if a first child dies. I know my husband and I would have succumbed to the statistical average.

I thought my nightmares would eventually dissipate, then disappear, but they come more frequently these days. They are a by-product of motherhood, companion anxieties to my fear of losing my son in the shopping mall, or of someone kidnapping him.

THE FIRE IS COMING. WE CAN FEEL THE HEAT, SEE THE BLACK SMOKE
BILLOWING AGAINST THE GREY SKY. I DIG TRENCHES ALL AROUND MY
HOUSE TO KEEP THE FLAMES OUT. MY SON AND I HIDE IN THE COLD
STORAGE ROOM. WE STARE AT A SPIDER CRAWLING OVER A JAR OF
SIX-YEAR-OLD APPLESAUCE. I WAIT FOR THE SOUNDS OF INTRUDERS.
MORE THAN RADIATION, I FEAR HARD, WILD-EYED MEN.

My editor's son is the same age as mine. I ask her if she has a photograph of him. She opens her briefcase and pulls out an elastic-bound packet. She spreads the photos on her polished oak desk, laying them down like Tarot cards. In the first photo he's a curly-blond toddler with a cautious smile and big eyes. Then he is a chubby lad with a wide grin. In the next photo he is bald and pale. Thin. He had leukemia, she explains as she picks up the photograph and examines it. In the next picture he has brown hair. His curls are gone. He is a different child.

My source phones me.

'It wasn't my son,' Joyce says. 'It was someone who had stolen his ID. The autopsy shows they weren't even the same height. It couldn't have been him.'

There is new resolve in her voice and for the first time in months she isn't in tears.

'But where's your son then?' I ask.

'I don't know,' she says, 'but that wasn't him.'

MADAWAN, ONT.—A LOCAL MAN WHO REPORTEDLY COMMITTED SUICIDE IN THAILAND LAST NOVEMBER MAY STILL BE ALIVE. JOYCE RICHTER, MOTHER OF STEVE RICHTER, 20, SAYS DISCREPANCIES IN THE AUTOPSY REPORT NOW PROVE THE BODY IN QUESTION IS NOT HER SON.

DROWNED

You glimpse her bloated, blue-tinged face as they pull her into the boat. That's all you see; it happens too quickly. You hesitate, lose your chance to take a photograph, though that is your job. Your editor will never know. Her long, mud-caked hair, adorned with silty lake weeds, hangs in clumps over the edge of the boat. No one needs to see that.

Her family's faces are frozen as she is pulled out of the lake. They do not cry, not yet. Her husband is still missing. Police divers pierce through the cold water, into the darkness below. Others trudge through the dripping forest, the prickly junipers, the naked maples, calling and calling, hoarse in the damp late fall air.

Drowned. Choked on water, mud. Here in this shallow lake. Really not a lake at all, just a man-made flood bay from the hydro dam.

You remember that storm three days ago. The same vicious winds that tore the leaves off your lilac tree capsized their boat, carried away their life jackets. She is your age. You imagined they would be found together, clutching, perhaps one drowning the other.

You find her grieving sister on the muddy shoreline. She said they loved each other. She is sure that her sister died a happy woman. Cold comfort: her corpse zipped into a black body bag.

Now you sit in front of your terminal doing your job, presenting the facts. But what is this objectivity? Is it a myth? Your monitor glows underwater green, taunting.

You type:

MADAWAN, ONT.—After three days of searching, a local woman's body was discovered late yesterday in a lake six kilometres northwest of this small town.

Her body. Yes, her bloated, blue body was found. But try telling that to those who loved Her, were looking for Her: their youngest daughter, their niece, their cousin. Searching for Her delicate hand, sketching children, Her rippling laughter. You write:

MADAWAN, ONT.—After three days of desperate searching, police divers pulled the body of a once-beautiful young woman out of an icy lake six kilometres northwest of this small town.

She was married only three months ago. You have been wooed and asked but are unable to decide. Paul says you can live together first. If you want. He bought a bungalow at Blue Lake, is always asking you to select wallpaper, tiles, shrubs. Details flood your mind at midnight—potentilla, willow patterns, faux marble—leaving no room for rest.

You find a photo of her in the files—a former beauty queen, a slender silver crown, a smile on her lips. Her fingers intertwined in a bouquet of red roses. You've seen her hands in the same pose, common lake weeds for her prize.

You scribble:

MADAWAN, ONT.—A talented, newlywed young woman has been found, drowned, in an icy man-made lake after three days of desperate, heartbroken searching. Her husband is still missing.

Paul works for Madawan Hydro. He operates the hydraulics or something—you have never been quite sure. He guided you through the hydro station once, but the gigantic generators oppressed, overwhelmed. You left, ran out an emergency exit, blinked in the sudden sunlight. He told you to come back in, held you in that tender spot just above your elbow. You said you wanted to go home.

Her husband was a lawyer. You've watched him in the courtroom badgering witnesses, speaking obsequiously to the judge, whispering to his clients in private hall corners. You did not trust him. Him and his soft Italian loafers. She trusted him to take her trolling. She knew nothing of the wilderness.

Paul wants you to marry him but you can't see it.

Her sister stood on the muddy shore, making circles with the toe of her shoe. She told you that her sister didn't want to go fishing, only did it to please him. You nodded, pretended to take notes. You look in your notebook now. The ink is smeared from rain. You have written the same three words again and again:

Drowning one another.

FRESH HELL OF
CHRISTMAS

'What's that smell?' Fiona demands as she steps into the kitchen accompanied by a swirl of frigid air.

'Can't you say hello like a normal person?' asks her mother, looking up from a half-finished cryptic crossword.

'Is something burning?' asks Fiona.

She kicks off her boots and leaps to open the oven door; acrid smoke billows out. She grabs the pot holder and pulls out a cookie sheet containing two halves of a butternut squash—and a paring knife, its plastic handle completely melted into the pan. Fiona opens the back door and runs out in her stocking feet, throwing the cookie sheet on top of the snow at the side of the deck. She comes back in and props the door open with her boot.

'Your oven is filthy, Fiona,' says her mom. 'You should clean it more often.'

'The oven's fine,' says Fiona, trying to stay calm.

She definitely did it, thinks Fiona as she takes off her socks and puts on her slippers. Typical of her not to take any blame.

'You left a knife by the squash,' she says, 'and it melted.'

'I certainly did not,' her mother retorts.

'I'm sure it was an accident, but you did, Mom. That's the smell: melted plastic.'

'Well, it wasn't me,' her mother says, going back to her crossword.

Normally, Fiona would let it go. She's the one who placates, who sooths the rough patches in their family dynamics, but this time, she's had it. Mom's lying, thinks Fiona. She should admit it and apologize.

'Mom, you were the one who put the squash in the oven. I just walked in the door, so it obviously wasn't me.'

'Maybe Neil was poking at it to see if it was done. Neil!' she shouts. 'Neil!'

'Where is he?' Fiona asks.

'Playing on the computer like always. Neil! Get down here!'

'Mom, stop bellowing! He's not five years old! He's a grown man.'

'Well, he doesn't act it, as you well know. Still living at home at thirty-four. It's shameful.'

'And he's not "playing" on the computer, he's working. He designs websites.'

'Why do you have to contradict everything I say?'

'What's up?' asks Neil.

'Hey, Neil.'

'Did you leave a knife in the oven, Neil?' asks their mother.

'No,' he says, looking confused. 'Why would I do that?'

'You weren't poking at the squash to see if it was done?'

'I've been upstairs working. What's that smell?'

'Overdone plastic,' Fiona says. 'Mom left a paring knife beside the squash in the oven and it melted.'

'It wasn't me,' says her mom.

Fiona throws her hands up.

'Look, forget it,' she says. 'No harm done. I've got lots of knives and we can have broccoli instead of squash.'

She shivers and closes the back door, but opens the window a crack. The smell still lingers, fills her nostrils.

'Luc will be home in a minute,' she says. 'He's making chicken marsala.'

'I can cook the chicken,' says her mom. 'Why do you make Luc do all the cooking? He's had a hard day at work.'

'So have I,' says Fiona. 'And I don't *make* Luc do the cooking, he likes it. It relaxes him. Besides, he doesn't do all of it. I do a lot on the weekend, and I bake.'

'I never let your dad cook,' says her mother, shaking her head.

'Yeah, and look how well that turned out,' says Neil.

There is a moment of frigid silence. Uh-oh, thinks Fiona, now we're in for it.

'What do you mean by that?' comes the icy retort from their mother.

'Cool your jets, everyone,' says Fiona. 'How about a pre-dinner glass of wine? I have a very nice bottle from Rufina.'

She gets out three glasses. Family lubricant, she thinks.

'Sorry, Mom,' says Neil mechanically. 'I didn't mean anything.'

'If you haven't got something nice to say, then don't say anything at all,' their mother declares.

Fiona hands them each a glass of ruby-coloured wine. Apropos of nothing, her mother says: 'Did I tell you about my friend Agnes?'

'Your friend from the Madawan bridge club, right?' asks Fiona, relieved to be talking about anything other than that damned knife.

'Yes, that's right. Well, her friend Dorothy hurt her shoulder doing something, I'm not sure what, but she didn't get it seen to. And then last week she goes out into her yard to fill the bird feeder, slips on the ice and breaks her hip. And because of her damaged shoulder she couldn't move. Three days later she was found. Dead from exposure.'

'That's terrible!' says Fiona.

'What are you insinuating?' asks Neil.

Fiona gives him a sharp look.

'Nothing. Just telling a story,' says their mother.

'Not a cautionary tale?' asks Neil.

'Well, I think she was a very silly woman for not getting her shoulder looked after. It might have saved her life,' says their mom.

'Enough of this cheerful talk,' says Fiona, forcing a smile to her face and raising her glass: 'Here's to our family reunion.'

They clink glasses.

And now for the fresh hell of Christmas, thinks Fiona. Why do I invite them every year?

FUNERAL
HATS

We all own the hats we'd planned to wear to our husbands' funerals. We don't need the hats now—all five of us are divorced or separated—but we keep them anyway.

We sit in Sheila's living room, talking about men as we plunge into the fourth bottle of decent vintage Italian wine. We've all read the same analysis of eighteen studies in the *Journal of Personality and Social Psychology*, showing conclusively that married men are the happiest, married women the least happy. None of us are shocked; we agree with these findings. I cite another study indicating that married women do more housework than single mothers because, despite good intentions, husbands *make* more work than they *do*.

'What is it with men anyway?' says Kate, launching into the classic complaint. 'After so many years of practice, they still can't hit the toilet bowl. You'd think they were trying to aim a shotgun from a hundred feet.'

The howls of laughter die down; wind rattles the windows.

For me, it began in passion and ended in indifference. It's impossible to pinpoint the beginning of this evolution, the final devolution. There were myriad arguments, a plethora of innuendos and miscommunications.

Me trying to justify my youthful promiscuity (again). I used to think that relationships demanded honesty, full disclosure. Now, after seven years of marriage, I think Ann Landers is right: what happened before is nobody's business. I sigh and tell my husband that it was the norm during the pre-AIDS, post-pill era. The '70s heyday of singles' fern bars and sweaty discos ('push, push in the tush').

'Lots of people were doing it,' I say. 'It was a time of free love and you missed the boat.'

'You slut!' he growls.

The years have made me immune to his insults, but I'm honestly perplexed by this reaction. I didn't mean to offend; I was just offering the facts. Then I realize his maleness is threatened because I'm more sexually experienced. At one time I would have tried to temper my words with an elaborate explanation. Now I know it is futile. No matter what I say he will use my words as ammunition in the daily fusil-lade. 'This is your problem,' I say. 'Don't make it mine.'

For the first time, I refuse to get back in bed with him. I stumble down the dark hallway and curl up next to my sleeping son. He cuddles against me, his regular breathing lulling me to sleep.

I'm shocked that we have these hats. It's so demented. One by one all five of us assert that we didn't really want our husbands dead.

'It was a crazy sort of daydream,' says Patty. 'I always felt guilty after-wards.'

'The way I figured it,' says Sheila, 'it would be easier if he did die. Widows get a lot more sympathy than divorcées. I could have saved face. Not to mention lawyer's fees.'

I stare at her. 'Don't look at me like that,' she says. 'It was only a fantasy.'

Some of the hats are quite plain: broad-brimmed straw, felt pillbox. Mine is vintage, plush black velvet with a cascading three-foot veil. I bought it at a rummage sale because I liked the idea of my face beneath black netting, hiding my expression, my emotions. It soon became my fantasy funeral hat, its veil concealing my dry, bright eyes. Now it hangs on a picture hook in my bedroom, collecting dust.

I stayed in the marriage for the sake of my baby boy. He rests behind turquoise cur-tains in the semi-darkness and stifling heat, dreaming of piggyback rides and chasing the kitty and 'pretty, pretty' roses that my friend Nancy gave me for looking after her daughter.

My husband comes into my office and caresses my lower back, asks if I want to go and 'rest' for a while. I flick my computer on, saying I have work to do. I can't bring myself to touch him; I cringe when he touches me.

Heather is the first to confess. 'He'd never phone when he was going to be late getting home. I used to worry. I'd imagine he'd been in a car accident. Then I wondered what would happen if he died.'

A few women nod; others concur aloud. We, too, had imagined quick, relatively painless deaths. An airplane crash, a car hit by a freight train, a plunging elevator. And we each confess that we'd planned the funerals with the sprays of red roses and a selective guest list. We'd planned the menu for the reception including pâté de fois gras and fine sherry. We'd envisioned our outfits. Bought hats. I feel as if I've been let into some sinister fraternity (or is it maternity?). I recall a story about a woman who poured nail polish remover on her husband's penis and set it on fire. He didn't press charges.

The snow continues to blow against the window but the room is suddenly too warm. I pull at my turtleneck, then down my glass of red wine.

After a day of rifts and ruptures, my husband comes to bed at midnight. I rustle under the covers, half-awake. He asks: 'Do you still love me?' I hesitate. Every passing moment stabs us. He asks me again: 'Do you still love me?' I say: 'I'm not sure.' (Trying not to say anything, trying to break it to him gently.)

'How long have you known?' he asks.

'Not long,' I whisper hoarsely.

He accuses me of having an affair. I deny it, but I know he doesn't believe me. I say I am sorry, say I want to make things as easy as possible for him. He says he should have known better than to marry someone like me. I don't ask what he means. He gets up to go sleep on the living room couch. I don't stop him.

Lying in bed afterward, I feel that large emptiness that comes at the end of a relationship that we began with such high hopes. The emptiness before the new begins.

The details vary among the five of us. As we tell our stories, our casts of characters ebb and flow through our consciousnesses leaving an emotional residue, a flotsam and jetsam. We seem to share everything, but I notice no one speaks of her dreams, of the things that matter now. Like me, they're waiting for their lives to settle.

I saw myself sipping coffee in trendy cafés with new literary friends, attending lectures and readings, and participating in lofty conversations. Instead, I am enmeshed in a daily tangle of housework, childcare and office politics. But at night I sprawl luxuriously under cool sheets, my reading light bothering no one.

I imagined that after the funeral rows of friends would line up to embrace me and murmur words of condolence. There are no friends lined up in divorce. On his side, allegiances have solidified. My married friends avoid me now, afraid that the dissolution of my marriage may be contagious. Like lepers, we divorcées keep our own company.

All five of us keep our hats. Heather's is tucked into an oval box under a grey felt fedora. Sheila's lies unceremoniously in a jumble of Halloween costumes. I've been thinking of putting mine away in my cedar chest, tucking it into the folds of my silk wedding dress. But I'm afraid that during the humidity of summer the black dye will bleed into the white.

PART THREE

Wanda in Five Times

COMET, IT TASTES LIKE GASOLINE

I run the last four blocks from school, crash through the back door and race down the basement stairs. I reach the cardboard box by the furnace, then freeze. A wad of my old flannel PJs are bunched up in a corner. Hair clings to it. But no kittens. No little kittens anywhere.

No use checking under the water heater or calling. I know what's happened. I race back upstairs to the kitchen, don't even realize I'm crying until Daddy says, 'Stop your blubbering, Wanda, or I'll give you something to cry about! They're only cats for god's sake.'

'We took them to the SPCA,' Mom says.

'But they were only four weeks old,' I whimper.

'Old enough,' Daddy decrees, and takes a drag off his cigarette.

'Someone will take them,' adds Mom. 'You knew you couldn't keep them.' She says it as if it's all my fault.

'They'll find proper homes for them,' adds Daddy.

I make it halfway down the basement steps, then collapse in tears, gasping in tight raspy whispers—'They're so mean ... no fair ... poor little things ...' My breath comes in short bursts and mucous clogs my throat. The basement door slams, catapulting me off the steps back to the laundry room. I step into the large packing box where Pippi Longstocking now lays on the flannel. I curl up beside her, whispering into her fur: 'They're okay, Pippi. I'm sure they have homes now, with kind children and good food and lots of petting. And no yelling.'

I kick the end of the box, breaking the cardboard. Kick and kick. Kick.

Dear Granny C,

How are you? I am fine. It rains every day and Mom says she wishes we'd never left Ottawa. They took Pippi Longstockings kittens to the SPCA and I'll never see them again and Pippi is very sad and so am I. Mom says there were too many. I wish I could have kept Pumpkin Pie with orange fur like her mama.

I finished The secret garden in only 4 days. I liked it except the end. What happens to the girl? I liked the part where everyone starts being nice to her. Someone is always mad at me. Did you get mad with Mom when she was 8? Do you know any other books I could find at the library? Mom and Daddy are having a going away party for Uncle Tim. He's moving to Edmonton. Write soon please.

Love, Wanda

———

Half-light. Half-dark. Twirling through Mom's party dresses, inhaling perfume memories of parties past, caressing lavender velvet. I rub my cheek against peony-red silk, light as a good-night kiss from Daddy. Except he never kisses me. 'My princess!' I imagine him whispering. I smile softly, sing: 'One little girl in a pale pink coat, Yodel-lay, yodel-lay, yodel-layee hoo! What do you get ...'

Sharp heels click up the stairs. I freeze against prickly white mesh. Dang double dang! I'm not allowed to mess in Mom's closet and there's no way out now without getting caught. I slide the door shut and collapse like a folding chair onto the floor beside the rows of shoes, under long skirts. I peer through the louvres. Mom walks by in her white mules with the pompoms on top—just like my Barbie's shoes—and sits at her little dressing table.

Please don't hear my heart beating, I think. I can just see the look on Mom's face, all disappointed, her sighing: 'Oh, Wanda. Why do you have to sneak around and spy on people? Why can't you behave like other little girls?'

Mom crosses her short, plump legs, examines her chin in the mirror and pokes at something with her tweezers. She's getting ready for their party—although she's already spent her usual hour in front of the mirror today primping and prodding. She wouldn't dream of going to the corner shop without full makeup. Not like Teresa's mother who goes grocery shopping wearing a chiffon scarf over her spongy pink curlers. Mom always looks nice. She changes into a dress before Daddy comes home and even wears colour-coordinated slacks and blouses to do housework. Our cleaning lady, Mrs Aruba, wears a faded housedress with the hem hanging. She does the hard stuff—scrubbing floors and cleaning windows—but Mom says there's still plenty to do with two children tracking dirt around. One time I watched her poking a toothpick into the little crack around a light switch, pulling out a thin line of dust. 'See,' she said, dangling it in front my eyes, 'it gets everywhere.' I nodded, trying to be nice but wondering why she bothers when it isn't even march-out time. That's when the men from the military housing office come to inspect the house with white gloves. They check everywhere, even behind the fridge, and if they find dirt, well, Mom says we could be kicked out of our PMQ. So Mom and Mrs Aruba tear the whole house apart. Pictures come down, walls are scoured, drapes are sent for cleaning, carpets shampooed, floors scrubbed, then waxed and buffed to a slippery shine. Every window polished.

'Winifred!'

Oh no, it's Daddy.

'I'm in here, Wayne,' Mom calls, putting down the tweezers and picking up a powder puff. 'In the bedroom.'

I pull away from the door, shrinking into the back of the closet. I'll really get in trouble if *he* catches me. My breathing seems so loud. Please don't hear me, please, I pray, biting the side of my index finger, which is already red and torn from nervous nibbling.

'You've spent way too much money as usual,' Daddy says. 'How much did all that booze cost anyway?'

I put my hands over my ears, but there's no way to shut out Daddy's booming voice—like the drill sergeant on *Gomer Pyle*, except Daddy's in the Royal Canadian Air Force. A navigator. Officer. 'Came up through the ranks,' I've heard him say a million times.

Mom puts down her puff and turns to Daddy. 'People will bring bottles, Wayne. It won't cost much, honey. Besides, Tim is your best friend. You can't let him move away without some sort of party. What would people think?'

'Maybe they'd see him for the Judas he is. I should have made major, not him.'

I hear him flick his Zippo to light up another Peter Jackson. 'He stole my promotion with all his kowtowing to the commandant, being his little errand boy.'

I risk all to peek through the louvres. Daddy takes a deep drag, then shakes his head in disgust, squinting his large brown eyes with the thick eyelashes. He's as handsome as a movie star. Mom's friends think so too. I heard the ladies from the Welcoming Committee giggling over afternoon sherry and saying how lucky Mom is to have such a good-looking husband.

Daddy takes a deep drag of his cigarette, inhales slowly. 'Wouldn't catch me brown-nosing like Tim.'

'You'll get your promotion too, dear. You've already done so well. We're all so proud of you. You just have to–'

'What the hell do you know about it?' His finger shoots out, cigarette dangling as he points at Mom. Mom! He never gets angry at her!

'Are you there in the briefing room at oh six hundred?' he yells. The veins on his forehead stand out. Dang double dang. I catch my breath.

'Have you seen *your* name gradually move down the duty roster?'

'No,' Mom murmurs, looking down at her hands.

'Well,' he growls. 'Then don't tell me what will and will not happen'—he bangs his fist on her dressing table, making the perfume and nail polish bottles rattle—'when you don't know a goddamn thing about it.'

He slams the bedroom door on the way out. I let my breath go. Mom never catches it like that! It's always me, or Ward. I'm glad it wasn't me. I always start crying when Daddy yells. And if he's really mad, he jabs his finger in my chest — 'you stupid, thoughtless girl' — and then I want to die, I feel so useless. My stomach aches just thinking about it.

I peek through the louvres again. Mom is staring at herself in the mirror. Then Dad comes back into the room, leans over and kisses the top of Mom's head. 'I didn't mean to yell at you,' he whispers.

I can't believe what I'm hearing.

Mom smiles at him in the mirror. 'That's okay, dear. You have every right to be disappointed about the promotion.'

'I'll make it up to you later,' he says, winking and flashing his perfect teeth as he leaves the room.

Mom wipes her eyes with a pink tissue, smiles at herself in the mirror, checks her lipstick, then goes into the bathroom. Now's my chance. I ease the closet door open, crawl onto the plush, rose carpet and pretend to examine the rows of shoes. I'm allowed to look at Mom's shoes and purses, even opening and closing them and playing with the little coin bags and mirrors inside. Mom comes back carrying a can of hairspray, sits at her dressing table and spies my reflection in her mirror.

'Oh, you startled me. Sit up straight, Wanda. Did you put out the napkins like I asked?'

I nod, but she's leaning into the mirror to inspect her hairdo.

'What are you wearing, Mom?'

'That old blue silk, what else?' she says sharply, then catches herself and speaks more softly. 'Wanda, will you please see if you can find my blue sateen shoes?'

She pats her high pile of curls and begins spraying it in place. I hold my nose. I'll never use that stinky stuff. I want hair like Granny C's: long grey-and-black hair that she magically coils into a tight bun, held tight with only four bobby pins.

'I think they're on the right side,' Mom adds.

The shoes are arranged in neat rows according to colour, some dyed specially to match dresses, purses. A real lady always has matching purse and shoes, Mom says. I inspect the shoes, run my fingers over the leather, suede and satin, singing under my breath.

One, two, buckle my shoe,
Three, four, shut the door
Five, six . . .

Last week, I brought the kittens into the closet and tried to put them in the shoes, but they kept climbing out and running away on their chubby legs. Little sweethearts. I matched their fur with the shoe: orange pump for Pumpkin Pie, black-and-white leather for Puss in Boots, soft grey suede for Rainy, and white spike heel for Snow White. I dressed them up in doll clothes, too—pink ruffles, blue bows and yellow jackets—though they scratched and squirmed. I still have a scratch on my hand from Pumpkin Pie, but she didn't mean to do it. Eventually I got them dressed and settled into my doll carriage. Up and down the front sidewalk I went, not daring to take them too far from home in case Carl, the big boy down the street, tipped over the carriage—or worse. Ward says Carl put a firecracker up a cat's bum and lit it.

It doesn't matter now. The kittens are gone to the SPCA.

'Do you think someone came and got my kittens yet?' I ask Mom.

She clicks her compact shut. Sighs. '*I* don't know, Wanda.' She busies herself twisting open gold and silver tubes of lipstick, comparing them to the red of her fingernail polish. She stops to light a Craven M. I inhale the minty smell.

'I think they've all got new homes,' I say brightly. 'They're so sweet. Especially little Pumpkin Pie. She was the sweetest. I wish . . .' But I stop myself. We've been through this before. Mom says I'm lucky to even have Pippi because Daddy doesn't like house cats.

'They do nothing to earn their keep,' he'd said. 'It's not like on the farm where the barn cats kept the mice out of the grain.'

'But they'll be good if we have a mouse in the house,' I'd said.

Daddy laughed. 'A mouse wouldn't find a crumb to eat here the way your mother cleans.'

I said nothing, just stared at my saddle shoes, thinking of how the kittens purred—like they were singing. I used to lie on my back and they'd all cluster around my head, purring, purring so loudly that I couldn't hear anything else. Not even Daddy.

I pull out the blue sateen shoes with their towering three-inch heels and slip one on for a moment. I know better than to try to stand up. I hate black-and-white saddle shoes. I wish I had black patent like Joan, the girl across the street, or better still, ballet slippers. Pink ones, with ribbons. I asked for ballet lessons but Mom said she doesn't have time to drive me around. Brownies is enough. I asked Daddy, too, but he said I'm too clumsy and then when I ran out of the kitchen, I banged my hip against the door jamb and got a big bruise. But I didn't cry. I try and try to be their pretty, polite, curly-haired daughter—the one they are always going on about—but I can't. I have knobby, banged-up knees and flyaway hair that won't stay put. My skirts twist, my leotards sag, my slips show and I always have some gunk on my face.

And on top of everything else, I'm bad. When Daddy yells or Mom gets all quiet and mean, I hide their things. Or break them. I slipped into Daddy's den and hid his favourite brush that he uses to paint his little metal soldiers. I put it down beside some paint on a lower shelf. After a few days, I put it back in the cup. I also broke his comb. Once, I ripped up Mom's shopping list and threw it under some bushes on the way to school. Sometimes I hide Mom's jewellery. Or her favourite lipstick. They always ask Ward or me if we've seen these things and I shake my head no. I know it's wrong but I can't help it.

'Wanda,' Mom says as she smooths on blue eyeshadow, 'don't say anything to your father about Uncle Tim's promotion, okay? He's not very pleased about it.'

'Okay, Mom.'

He's not really my uncle. He's Daddy's best friend, or at least he was. Now I don't know. But I love Uncle Tim. Sometimes he takes Ward and me bowling or to the movies— *The Sound of Music* twice, and *Old Yeller*. When he's visiting, he tells us a bedtime story made up out of his head, no book or anything. We cuddle up on either side of him on the couch and listen to stories about how he saved horses, dogs and old ladies from certain death.

I sit on the edge of Mom's bed. 'Does Daddy hate Uncle Tim?'

'No, of course not,' she says quickly. 'I don't know where you get these ideas from.'

I watch her spit into her red mascara box and vigorously move the brush back and forth, then lean into the mirror to apply it in short strokes, eyes opened wide. I open my eyes wide, too. Wide as I can.

————

A large white apron covers Mom's blue dress as she arranges the hors d'oeuvres. Horse's ovaries, Uncle Tim calls them. Mom holds her breath as the shrimp dip slips out of its mould with a glop into a perfectly shaped fish. She exhales and starts putting Ritz crackers around it.

'Can I help?' I ask.

'No, that's okay. I'll be done in a minute.' I stare at the hole in the big toe of my white sock; Mom doesn't trust me to do it right.

'You can open the chips, honey,' Mom says in her phony-bright voice—the voice she uses for company. 'Put them in the chip bowl on the table.'

Ward comes in with two cartons of pop. 'Where do you want these, Mom?'

'See if there's room in the fridge, Ward. If not, stick them under the kitchen table for now.'

Ward snatches a few chips from my bowl, stuffs them in his mouth and opens wide, mid-chew.

'Ward!' I protest.

'Nah, nah, nah, nah, nah, nah,' he taunts, showing off the half-chewed mess.

'Mom, Ward's chewing with his mouth open.'

'Stop it, you two, do you hear?'

Ward puts the bottles under the table.

I pop a chip into my mouth. How come I always get in trouble too?

Mom glances over at the sound of my crunching, but says nothing. There'll be lots of treats tomorrow morning. Ward and I will get up early and sneak into the living room. First we'll check under the couch cushions for change that has fallen out of pockets. Then there are the leftover party snacks: Cheezies, pretzels and chips—barely stale—and my favourite, cocktail peanuts. Ward will sip the dregs of highballs. Rye and Coke or ginger ale. Sometimes a gin and tonic. I tried a sip once but it was horrible. Sometimes we find cigarettes, too. Partial packs or some left in the brass cigarette holder. Ward takes them all, says they're for his friends, but I saw him smoking behind the Big Dawg's _tore—it's actually Store but the *S* fell off the sign so they call it the tore. I haven't said anything about him smoking.

Pippi is winding around my ankles. Poor Pippi. I sit cross-legged beside the kitchen table, nestling the cat in my lap. 'I'm sure they're okay, Pippi,' I whisper in her ear. 'I'll try to find out later. Maybe Uncle Tim could ask.'

'When's Uncle Tim coming?' I ask, but Mom doesn't seem to hear. Uncle Tim says I'm his special girl. He babysat a couple times and let me sit on his lap while we played Snakes and Ladders. And he made Ward and me laugh like maniacs.

'Ooooop going down, bargain basement,' he said. Then: 'Yeee coming up. Fourth floor, ladies' underwear.'

Once after he babysat, I heard my parents talking about him in the kitchen.

'He'd make a wonderful father,' said Mom.

'But he doesn't have that appeal with the ladies,' said Daddy. 'One disaster after another. Remember Judy? Nice girl, too.'

'I've been racking my brain trying to think of someone for him,' said Mom.

Pick me, pick me, I thought as I scampered back to my bedroom. I know I'm too young. Even the girl next door who's in college and has all the Beatles albums is too young. But Uncle Tim did call me his little sweetheart. He used to tickle me before bed and give me big bear hugs.

'It's a big bear come to get little Wanda,' he'd roar. And I'd hide, squealing, under the covers.

Not lately, though. Not since he met Didi, his girlfriend. Now he's too busy for us. And he's moving—transferred to Edmonton. Something about him training to be a wink commander. I can just see him winking and winking and grinning. He'll do a great job.

This is the wrong year for us; we won't be moving yet. I remember our other house, though Mom says there have been two since I was born. The last PMQ, in Ottawa, was almost the same as this one but the clapboard was painted pale blue and this one is white with ugly, faded brown trim. But at least my room is in the same place at the end of the hall—farthest away from the stairs in case a murderer comes in the middle of the night. I'll have a chance to jump out the window before he gets to me, even if I break my leg. It'll be worth it. Then I'll be an orphan like Pippi Longstocking, the strongest girl in the world.

Daddy comes rushing into the kitchen. 'You better get the lead out, Winifred. They'll be here any minute now.'

Mom wipes away a speck of shaving cream that's stuck to his cheek and smiles at him. 'I wouldn't mind a cocktail to get into the spirit.'

'I'll make them,' volunteers Ward.

I wish I'd offered first. Ward and I take turns mixing the drinks. They're always the same: rye and Coke. Three ice cubes, four fingers of Canadian Club if I'm making them—Ward only has to use three—then top it off with Coke and stir it with one of the swizzle sticks Daddy collects from hotels. That's the best part, fooling with Daddy's beer stein full of sticks from exotic places: Vancouver, Paris, London, Kenya, Washington, D.C. One, from the Tiki Club, is shaped like a woman, her boobs forming the handle. I sneak a slug of Coke too, if no one's around.

'No, I'll mix it myself, son. You help your mother,' Daddy says.

He marches into the living room and checks the bar Mom has set up, everything meticulously placed on a white linen cloth. I squish myself against the door frame, wanting to ask him if he thinks someone got the kittens, but I'm too afraid. He straightens the perfectly arranged bottles of gin, rye, vodka and rum with their little silver tags hanging around the necks even though the labels are plain as can be. He shifts around the bowls of bright red cherries, pickled pearl onions and lemon slices. He likes everything ordered just so. It's the same in his den where he paints his metal soldiers. His brushes are arranged in jars according to size and his paints are in a wire rack, arranged according to colour. His history books are organized alphabetically by author, with titles like *The Rise and Fall of the Third Reich* and *The Proud Tower*. Each book's dust jacket is wrapped in clear plastic Mactac to keep it clean. Two walls are covered with homemade, glassed-in shelves containing hundreds of little soldiers arranged in war scenes. Some of them depict battles from the American Civil War, the War of 1812 or the Napoleonic Wars but most are from World War II. Sometimes, when he's in a good mood, he lets me clean his brushes. I love the smell of the turpentine and standing next to him, asking him about the soldiers. He patiently tells me the dates of things and the strange-sounding names of battles in far-off places: Waterloo, Midway, Pearl Harbor. One Saturday last fall, he let me paint the green army fatigues on a German soldier and said I did a good job. I asked to help again the next week, but he said no, he was too busy to watch me every second.

His cigarette smokes between his lips as he rattles the ice bucket noisily and clicks the cubes into glasses. He pours a splash of rye in each glass. He spills a bit of Coke on the white cloth and shifts the bowl of cherries to cover it. He turns, holding the tinkling glasses: 'Don't stand there gawking, Wanda. Were you brought up in a barn?'

He says this all the time but he's the one who grew up on a farm in Saskatchewan during the Depression. We've heard the stories a zillion times. How they ate boiled fat and potato stew. How his mother died when he was six and his father blamed his two sons and his daughter for working her to death and eating more than their keep. Daddy says he quickly learned to 'buck up and be a man'. He says this glaring at Ward, and I'm really glad to be a girl. Daddy had to get up early to study before chores, and then walk three miles each way to school. He spent his summers haying and repairing tractors. The day he graduated from high school, he enlisted. His biggest regret is missing the war. That's what he tells his buddies when they drink beer in the backyard.

I wander out to the kitchen and spot the trays of hors d'oeuvres covered in plastic wrap. One tray has a little bowl of sardines with a stack of coloured toothpicks next to it. I lift the plastic wrap and poke at one of the sardines. It's soft and slimy. I pull the wrap down as Mom comes in. 'Stop fooling with that, Wanda. It's time for your PJs and teeth. You can read for twenty minutes but lights out at eight-thirty. I'll be checking.'

'Can't I stay up a bit, Mom? Just till people start to come so I can see the clothes and stuff?'

'It's a grown-up party, dear—you'll only be bored. Your father wants you and Ward out of the road.'

I sigh. This is definitive. I could argue with Mom, plead and cajole, but not with Daddy. He never changes his mind. Not about anything. Even when it's not fair.

Daddy starts the record player in the living room. I recognize the music from *The Bridge on the River Kwai* and sing along as I button my PJs:

Comet, it tastes like gasoline

Comet, it makes your face turn green

Comet, it makes you vomit

So have some Comet and vomit today

Those aren't the real words. I learned them from other air force brats after family mess dinners. We play in the lounge—hiding behind heavy curtains and bounding over leather-upholstered furniture—while our parents drink coffee and cognac and smoke cigarettes in the dining room.

I don't like being called a brat. I'm not spoiled, and I at least try to be good. The other kids at the dinners are brats. Real brats. The girls in my class never go; it's just the younger kids. They slurp their soup, talk with their mouths full, spill their milk, eat with their hands. But not Ward and me—we eat properly. Like grown-ups. One good thing though: after the parents are finished their coffee, we get to watch a movie on a screen at the end of the dining room. Good ones, too, like

It's a Mad, Mad, Mad, Mad World. During the funny parts, Daddy laughs louder than anyone else.

No one will notice if I don't brush. I crawl into bed, surround myself with my stuffed animals—my protectors against the night. Nights are the worst, the darkest, the scariest. You never know what's hiding in the closet or under the bed. Joan across the street is allowed to have a night light. It's shaped like a doll and glows pink against her wall. Not me though. I'm not allowed. It's lights out and Mom firmly shuts the door, though I always slip out of bed afterward and open it a crack.

'Wanda,' Mom calls down the hallway, 'I forgot to tell you that a letter came from Granny today. It's on your dresser.'

I tumble out of bed, tangled in the sheets, and rip open the letter.

————

My little dear,

Wanda, I'm writing just a quick note before I pack for my holiday to Texas to see your great-aunt Rose. She lives in a wonderful house near the border of Mexico. I hope you and your mother and I can all go there some day and drink iced tea on her back patio surrounded by huge cacti (that's plural for cactus) and yucca plants.

You asked if I used to get angry with your mother. Of course I did, although I tried not to, but it never stopped me from loving her. I know your parents love you too, Wanda.

Your mother told me they couldn't keep all your kittens. I'm so sorry, Wanda. I know how well you looked after them and how much you loved them. I know it's hard for you to see right now, but maybe it's for the best. Now they'll each have their own loving home, and just think of all the joy they'll bring to those families. Don't fret, my little dear.

I'm glad to hear you liked *The Secret Garden.* I thought it was very nicely written. Have you read the Narnia series yet? There are seven books altogether but the best one is *The Lion, the Witch and the Wardrobe.* One of the main characters is a young girl named Lucy who is kind and brave and reminds me of you. I will mail you that book when I get home from vacation.

Meanwhile, I will send you and Ward postcards from Texas. Take care, little dear, be good and look after your mother.

Love always for you especially,
Granny C

———

I lie in bed, smiling as the first car crunches along the gravel driveway. Mom forgot to tuck me in, so that means I can get out of bed. Secretly, because as soon as Mom sees, it'll be lights out for sure. I sneak down the hall to the landing and peek down to the foyer below. Uncle Tim comes in with Didi, who is wearing a long gold gown, a see-through wrap draped around her bare shoulders. Her black hair is stacked high and glimmers with a gold hair band. Gosh, she's glamorous, like a movie star. I frown. More like Bette Davis in *Hush... Hush, Sweet Charlotte* that we saw at the drive-in. We weren't allowed to look when the head got cut off and bounced down the stairs, but I peeked around the edge of Daddy's seat and I saw. Didi's probably awful like that too. Beating up on crippled old ladies. Pushing people down the stairs.

'My god, you are one lucky man, Tim,' Daddy says. He gives Didi a long kiss on her cheek, his hands planted on her hips, then draws back. 'I'm surprised you made it out of the house.'

Uncle Tim chuckles, puts his arm around Didi's waist. Poor Mom. She'll never look as beautiful as Didi. Not even in her new pink suit that she said cost a-week's-groceries-but-don't-tell-Daddy. Mom's hands are clasped in front of her, a smile on her pale face.

'You are simply stunning, Didi,' continues Daddy. 'You better keep your eye on her, Tim!' he says, giving him a big wink. 'I may have to steal her away.'

Didi—what a stupid name. A prissy little kid's name or some dopey girl on Walt Disney.

Didi laughs, blushes. 'You're just awful, Wayne.' She untwirls her wrap and hands it to Mom, like she's a maid or something. Drop it, Mom! I whisper-wish. Just drop it! Or throw it in her face. But she doesn't. She carefully smooths the material, folds it and places it on the shelf above the coats.

Uncle Tim takes Didi's hand. 'We're making an announcement later tonight,' he says, grinning at her.

Didi blushes again and gives Tim a fake slap on his forearm. 'Tim, don't spoil the surprise.' He brushes her cheek with his lips. She pats her hair in case he's mussed it. As if he could with all that hairspray.

'Tim tells me you have some kittens,' she says. 'Can I see them?'

I hold my breath.

'You just missed them,' says Daddy. 'We took them to the SPCA.'

'Had them put to sleep,' adds Mom.

Daddy glares at her.

'Well, no one wants kittens these days,' Mom says.

I slump against the wall. Put to sleep! Dead. That's what it means, I know because Joan's dog was put to sleep last year after he got hit by a car. They're dead. I clench my fists. Put to sleep! That's not what they told me. Liars! Liars! I rock back and forth on my heels, banging my head softly against the wall. Mom and Dad are liars and if I had half Anne Shirley's gumption I'd tell them what I think. I'd tell them they're big fakes.

The doorbell rings. I wipe away my tears with my arm, take a deep breath and slip down the hallway, into the gleaming bathroom. The guest towels are carefully folded, embroidered hand towels arranged just so on the counter.

I throw the towels on the floor, stomping on them. 'They're all stupid.' I turn the sink taps on and splash water on the counter, floor and hand towels, soaking them. 'I'll teach them to kill my kitties.' I rub some of Mom's smelly Chantilly Lace hand lotion on the towels. Put to sleep, Mom said. And Uncle Tim with his arm around Didi's waist. And Dad winking. I squeeze toothpaste on my brush and smear it on the sink and mirror, catching a glimpse of my red, ugly face. I lean in closer for a better look: squinty, red-rimmed eyes, huge blotchy nose, fat lips. This is me, this is who I am. Stupid girl.

I yank open the mirrored door and peer into the medicine cabinet. Ex-Lax chocolate. Mom gives it to me sometimes; constipation runs in the family on Dad's side, she says. I unwrap the new bar and stuff the whole thing in my mouth, chewing the big gob. It's horrible, waxy. Not like chocolate at all. Brown spit dribbles out of the corner of my mouth. I wipe it on a pale blue guest towel. I leave the wrapper on the counter where Mom will be sure to see it. I'll get sick and ruin the party and it serves them right. I run to bed, pull the blankets over my head and wait in the half-dark.

PEELING
THE ARTICHOKE

Sandy McCaffrey says they have to move out of their house so the Sullivans can move back in. 'Mrs Sullivan wants to die there,' Sandy whispers in my ear, even though we're alone in my bedroom and no one's around. The house on Russell Road is Mrs Sullivan's favourite out of all the houses in all the postings they've had. That's what Sandy says. They, the Sullivans, have five kids, and the mother, she has cancer. Maybe it's because she had all those kids. I beg Sandy for details and she tells me about an open sore oozing green stuff. She's a liar but I listen anyway.

The day the Sullivans move in we gather behind Mr Neilson's side fence, watching out for Tonto, his fat, slobbering bulldog with the pink eyes. Sandy and my brother, Ward, and I peek through the slats at the Sullivans' house. It's the biggest and best in the neighbourhood—it used to be part of the convent across the street. It's the nuns' old house and there's still a wrought-iron fence along the front, but the gate is gone and just the hinges are left.

Most of the houses around here belong to US Air Force officers who want to retire here in Colorado Springs someday—that's what Dad says. Meanwhile they rent their homes to other military families. We're one of the families that rents. It's better than living on the base in a PMQ because the houses and yards are bigger. It's the same in a way too, since most of the kids are army brats. But living in the States is weird. The other kids come from places like Montgomery, Alabama, or Brownsville, Texas. They've never heard of Penhold, Alberta, or Trenton, Ontario. The rules are weird too. Mom warns us over and over about rattlesnakes in the fields and black widow spiders hiding in cracks in the bluffs behind the convent.

'Lookit,' Sandy says, pinching my upper arm. She's always pinching my arms and legs, leaving red marks, bruises. 'Lookit, a maid!' We see a coloured woman going into the house. No one else has a maid. 'Rich snobs,' Sandy mutters.

'Maybe it's because of their mom,' I say. 'Someone to look after the kids and stuff.'

'Sssh,' hisses Ward, 'or get lost.'

'Shut up, ya fat moron,' says Sandy.

He doesn't say anything back even though he's two years older and could beat the snot out of her. He's such a chickenshit.

'Where's the mother?' I whisper.

Sandy shrugs.

We see the father come out of the house, real quiet, not yelling or bossing the kids. He goes into the moving van and comes out with a gold floor lamp. Dad never helps the moving guys. When we moved here last summer he said, 'That's their job. I don't ask them to help navigate a plane.'

I don't see how the Sullivans will ever get their house set up even if Colonel Sullivan does help, because it's Mom who does the real work when we move. By the end of the first day, she has our beds made and sheets tacked up over the windows, dishes put away, lawn furniture put out. I'm getting good at it, too. I arranged my bedroom nearly the same as my old one in Trenton. And I got the last room at the end of the hall again—farthest from the door.

I rest my forehead against the fence slats and see the most beautiful girl—tall, red hair glimmering to her waist, pale skin and long, long legs. She looks seventeen, sixteen anyway. She talks to the packing men, pointing here and there. Then she calls all the kids and gives them chores. There's a blond girl who could be around my age, eleven or so, though she's smaller than me. Her hands are in her pockets and she's looking at the ground, tracing a pattern in the gravel with the toe of her sneaker.

———

The next morning I ride my bike up and down the steaming tarmac on Russell Road singing under my breath in time to the pumping pedals —

> *There's a log in the hole in the bottom of the sea,*
> *There's a log in the hole in the bottom of the sea,*
> *There's a hole, there's a hole, there's a hole in the bottom of the sea.*
> *There's a bump on the log in the hole in the bottom of the sea. . . .*

I race back down the road and see the Sullivan girl, the one who might be my age, sitting in her driveway trying to fix a tire on a beat-up bike.

'Hi,' I say. 'I can never fix a flat. Dad tells me I have to, but I can't do it.'

She smiles. 'It's way too hard. I just thought I'd try. Everyone's so busy.'

Her golden hair is spun into tiny curls and she has clear blue eyes, a wee turned-up nose and ears like tiny oval Barbie suitcases. Not like my lugs. That's what Dad calls them. Lugs — Scottish for big ears.

'I'm Rachel,' she says.

'Wanda,' I reply. 'I live two doors down.'

'Hey, wanna see my tree house?' she asks, putting the wrench down. 'Dad built it when we used to live here before, when I was a baby.'

I know the tree house. I've been up there a million times with Sandy — though she called it a tree fort and was always saying she was going to push me out, so I never wanted to stay long. For some reason I pretend to Rachel that I've never been up there. I admire the sturdy ladder and, at the top, the big wide platform with the railing all around and the little playhouse. It even has a window with red gingham curtains.

'Should I get my Barbies?' she asks.

'Sure,' I say, though I haven't played with mine for ages.

She comes back with a huge basket — more Barbie stuff than I've ever seen. 'You're so lucky,' I say.

'Most of it's my sisters' but they're too old now.'

'I wish I had a sister,' I say, picking up a shimmery gold nightclub dress. 'Except then Dad would boss her around too.'

'Is he mean?' Rachel asks, her eyes wide.

'No,' I say quickly, 'he just gets mad sometimes.'

I'm such an idiot telling her about Dad. What will she think?

'Which doll do you want?' she asks.

Sandy never asks me which doll I want—she takes the new one and leaves me the one whose feet have been chewed up by Titan, her horrible German shepherd who is always sticking his nose between my legs. I don't play Barbies with her anymore.

I take the second-best one, with short brown hair, leaving the newest one with the fancy blond hairdo for Rachel.

Rachel and I meet in the tree house the next morning and the day after, and the day after that—every morning. It's our place. Her sisters are too old for it and her brothers are building their own Rube Goldberg fort way on the other side of the yard. We play Barbies, making up stories where Ken is always proposing and one Barbie is always hesitating for one reason or another while her friend offers advice. And we read aloud, mostly from the book of fairy tales my Granny sent me. I bring over my *Anne of Green Gables* book too—none of these American girls have read it. When I showed it to Sandy she said it looked boring and wouldn't even try a chapter, but Rachel loves it.

'We're just like those kids in the book,' she says, 'all alone with just each other for company.'

One of the best things about the tree house is that it's perfect for spying. We can see straight into the upstairs bedroom windows, plus all the side and backyards. We can see where the boys are hiding for hide-and-seek and we make fun of the other kids as they race around looking for them. The deliverymen come and go: milk, bread, groceries, Colonel Sullivan's dry-cleaned uniforms and shirts. One day, we see her brother John's penis when he takes a pee by the side of the garage. There it is plain as day. I have a brother, too, but I've never seen that. Rachel says she's seen plenty. Even her father's once when his dressing gown fell open by accident.

'It was hu-ge,' she moans, and we giggle hysterically.

In the middle of the morning we always go down to the kitchen for a snack. Mom keeps our counters clear except for the toaster with its flowered cover, but their kitchen is big and messy. The turquoise countertops are covered in stuff: mixing bowls and mending, polishing cloths and tins full of freshly baked cookies. At home we aren't allowed to help ourselves to treats, but Rachel says Rosie—the maid who sleeps in a little room off the side of the kitchen—doesn't mind. We stuff handfuls of cookies into a paper sack—that's what they call it instead of a bag—then we fill a scratched, green thermos with purple Kool-Aid.

We go to the tree house every day except Sunday when the Sullivans go to mass.

'We're Catholic,' Rachel explains, 'that's why all our names are from the *Book of Saints*.'

I nod, though I've never heard of the book and I don't understand how Catholics are different from Presbyterians. We all believe in God, don't we? Except we don't go to church. Whenever Mom mentions going to church, Dad says, 'There's only one true religion: the military.' Then he laughs. All the Sullivans go to mass expect the mom because she's too sick. Too sick even to look after the kids. The oldest daughter, Mary, is in charge of the youngest children, Rachel and Joe, and the older two just do as they please while their mother lies in her bed in a tiny downstairs room. We watch the nurse arrive every morning to wash her and stuff; the kids have to be quiet and are only allowed to visit for a few minutes at a time. But when their father's at work Rachel has to tell their mother whenever she goes outside the yard. It doesn't really matter because Rachel has to tell Mary where she's going, too, but it's the rule and grown-up rules hardly ever make sense.

One day, before we leave to ride our bikes to the store for red Tootsie Pops—our favourite candy—Rachel pleads with me to come into her mother's room with her.

'I'll just wait here,' I say, leaning against the hallway.

'No, come in with me. Mom likes to meet my friends.'

'I dunno …'

'Please?' Then she whispers, 'You don't know what it's like, Wanda. I'm scared by myself.'

I'm the one who's afraid. Afraid of the dark. Afraid of things under my bed, in my closet. I want to be like Jo in *Little Women*. I cried when she cut her beautiful hair to buy medicine for her little sister. I imagined her hair falling to the ground and Jo looking straight ahead, seeing only what had to be done. I want to do something like that. I stand up straight and nod at Rachel.

It takes a few minutes for my eyes to adjust to the darkened room after the bright Colorado sunlight. The room is nearly empty; there's only one hard wooden chair in the corner and a small dresser with a few medicine bottles on top — no rugs or pictures. There's a single bed with a white, shiny cover, the outline of a long, thin body stretched out underneath. Her pale face is topped with a purple scarf instead of hair. I notice that her eyes are closed.

'Mom,' Rachel says. 'Mom, this is my friend, Wanda. She lives two doors down.'

'Hello, Wanda,' she says softly, blinking her eyes half-open.

'Glad to meet you, Mrs Sullivan,' I say in my best good-manners voice. I try to meet her eyes like Dad says I should, but I can't. I look at a small crucifix over her bed — the only thing hanging on the walls. There's blood coming from Jesus's hands and feet, trickling down his forehead. Suddenly I realize it really stinks in the room. Too much perfume, medicine or something I don't want to know about. I hope my mom never gets sick. Not ever.

I used to think Rachel was like the heroines in those fairy tales where the mothers die: Cinderella, Snow White, Hansel and Gretel. The girls are brave and adventurous and their mean stepmothers make them suffer for a while though they wind up happy in the end. But those are just stories. Rachel's mother is dying for real. I can't tell her I'm afraid too.

I watch Rachel kiss her mother's cheek and I want her to be my friend forever.

After that whenever I go with Rachel to visit her mother, I stand in the doorway and say hello, all the while inside I'm thinking of one of my favourite songs from Girl Scouts:

Make new friends,
But keep the old,
Some are silver and the others are gold.

————

I never call at Sandy's new house, even though it's just around the corner. And when she comes to my house I hide in the basement and don't answer when Mom calls. Or I slip out the back door, around the side, to the Sullivans' even if it means catching hell for not telling Mom where I'm going. I don't hate Sandy, but she isn't very nice. She's always running here or there like a crazy person, switching games all the time—Operation, then jacks, then Monopoly—until we wreck her bedroom, or mine, with every toy we own on the floor. She never helps clear up. And if I don't play what she wants, she kicks me. Ward kicks me too—under the table at dinner—but that's different; he's my brother.

Plus Sandy steals. She stole my Barbie stuff: a blue evening dress, red pillbox hat and pink mule slippers with pompoms. I could never prove it but I know she did, so I took her purple Barbie clutch bag. Just slipped it into my shorts pocket when she wasn't looking. We stole things last year in Mrs Piaget's grade five class: a plastic elephant from the zoo diorama, some new pencil crayons. I knew it was wrong, but then Sandy said I was a yellow-bellied Canadian coward so I had to do it. I came home and snuck a slug of Dad's Pepto-Bismol from the top shelf of the pantry. I'm glad I don't have to play with her anymore.

————

The summer days drag by, always sunny, always hot. It never rains here. Cacti and yucca grow in the yards. Dad's home most of July. Normally he's away on some trip or another and I used to feel glad when he went, then glad when he came home again. But here in Colorado it doesn't matter so much because he leaves us alone most of the time—hasn't given either Ward or me the strap since we moved here. He's always busy in his den or with his new friends. Mom and Dad go out all the time—four or five nights a week to cocktail parties, receptions and dinners. Or they have people over for dinner or drinks and cards. They haven't made friends with the Sullivans, though Mom sends over a giant casserole every week and encourages me to be friends with Rachel. 'Poor little muffin,' she calls her. The other good thing is that Mom and Dad don't fight about money anymore. They have an overseas allowance. That's what they call it but I don't understand because we didn't cross any oceans when we moved here. Dad finally goes on a trip at the beginning of August for two weeks. Sometimes when he comes home from a long trip he brings us a present—usually something from the airport gift shop, like a back scratcher or plastic fan. Once he gave me a stuffed tiger but it was the kind you attached to your car's turn signals so its eyes blinked when you turned right or left. Mom cut the wires off but the ends still poked out and the red glass light-bulb eyes glowed in the dark. It was scary and you couldn't cuddle or sleep with it. But this time when he comes home, he brings me a little gold ring with a pink stone. He's never bought me anything so nice. My first real jewellery. He brought one for Mom too—one with a real stone, a garnet. Mom says mine's fake. I don't care. It's beautiful, even if it is a bit too big for me. Mom says I should put it on a string around my neck so I won't lose it, but I put it on my fattest finger and go out to play.

———

By the end of summer, when the boys finally get tired of catching horned toads and lizards in the bluffs, when our flip-flops are pocked with holes from the burs we've pulled out over the past months, when all our toys are limp or broken, hair tangled, wheels missing, the boys decide to start a war. They've built two forts now, one on either side of the weed-filled garden, and spend a whole day making catapults. The next day they start launching clods of dirt and water balloons at each other and capturing prisoners. Rachel and I ignore them; we're organizing Barbie's wedding shower. After a summer of dates and fights, Ken has finally proposed and Barbie has accepted. Just when all the presents and fake food are set up for the wedding shower, a water balloon comes flying through the window, hits the opposite wall and sprays everything.

I spring to the window. 'Stop it, you guys!' I yell, but there's no one in sight. Suddenly another balloon smacks the side of the window, soaking my blouse. Then Rachel's brother John pops up from behind the trash can and goes peeling around the side of the house, laughing like a maniac. Tears come to my eyes. 'You jerk!' I scream.

He pokes his head around the corner of the house. 'Waa, waa, Wanda,' he calls. 'Afraid of a little water?'

As Rachel tugs at the bottom of my shorts, I crouch down. 'Let's turn the hose on them,' she whispers. I grin. I knew she wouldn't let them get away with it. We hurry down the ladder to the side of the house where the hose lies in a tangled heap. Without a word, we straighten it and Rachel takes it to the side of the house, close to one of the forts. She signals and I turn the water on full blast and run to her side. She gets them real good but then they come after us and she drops the hose and we start running to the front of the house. They catch us before we can get inside and pelt us with water balloons. I feel like I'm going to cry but then Rachel starts laughing, and I laugh too. The cold water feels good on my hot skin. We laugh until all their balloons are gone and then we can't stop laughing, tears running down our cheeks.

I'm washing my hands before setting the supper table when … my ring! It's gone! Dad'll kill me. I sneak back outside, run to the tree house, up the ladder—Rachel is long gone. I find a red Barbie slipper but no ring. On my hands and knees, I search in the grass underneath the tree. I walk to the side of the house by the hose, to the front where we got pelted. Nowhere. It's gone. And I can't look anymore because it's really supper-time now.

'Wanda!' says Mom. 'Where have you been? Go wash up—supper's ready. And you missed your turn to set the table, so you'll have to do two days in a row.'

My stomach roars. I want some Pepto-Bismol so bad. I down my food as quickly as possible so Dad won't yell at me for lingering. As I put down the dessert bowls of Jell-O at each place, he asks, 'Where's your ring?'

'In my bedroom,' I whisper, the words catching in my throat like minnows in a net. Just my luck for him to notice it's gone when I haven't even had time to look for it properly.

'Go get it.'

I drag my feet to my bedroom, supper a lump in the pit of my stomach. I open my jewellery box—a golden-velvet Canadian Club box—hoping the ring has magically appeared there. It hasn't. I close the box and go back to the dining room.

'I can't find it.'

'Your mother told you to put it on a string, but would you listen? No. And now you've lost it. Go to your room. I'll come when I'm finished.'

I know what this means. Ward sticks his tongue out at me as I leave the dining room. We both know what it means. I sit on the edge of my bed and wait for his footsteps. I hate him. I wish he'd go away and never come back.

'Pull down your pants and panties, bend over the bed,' he says, and I start crying before he even begins hitting me. He doesn't hit hard or anything and he only does it three times, but I cry anyway. All I can think is that I'm too old to be showing my bum to him.

Instead of knocking on Rachel's door the next morning, I go straight to the tree house and sit in a corner, arms wrapped around my knees. Why am I so careless? Why can't I be like the other girls—careful and pretty and obedient? Why didn't I listen to Mom?

'Wanda? Are you up there?' Rachel calls.

'Yeah,' I say.

She pokes her head up through the trap door. 'Why didn't you come to the house and get me?' I burst into tears, and tell her about the ring and the strap.

'On my bare bum!' I cry.

'Oh, Wanda, that's awful. My dad uses a ruler on the hand. But he hasn't for a long time. Does it hurt still?'

I shake my head no, savouring her sympathy, my misery. Fresh tears flow down my cheeks.

'Don't cry, Wanda. Please.'

I wipe my nose on my blouse.

'I know something that'll make you feel better,' she says.

'What?

'Well, you can't tell ever. It's a secret, okay?'

I nod.

'I call it rubbing,' she says.

'Rubbing?'

'Yeah, I do it sometimes when I'm sad. It's fun. You have to take off your pants and I'll take off mine and then you rub.'

'I guess,' I say slowly. 'But what if someone comes?'

'We'll wrap the blanket around us. No one's gonna come up here. They never do.'

She pulls off her faded blue shorts and I pull off mine. We stand there in our identical white panties—except the elastic is a little torn at the top of hers.

'Well?' I say. 'You first.'

She whips off her panties and throws them on top of her shorts. I do the same. It's not like I've never seen another little girl before, but I've never been allowed to stare. And how can you see your own parts? Our only full-length mirror is in Mom's bedroom and I'm not allowed in there since I broke Mom's shepherd lady figurine. I said it was an accident but it wasn't. I was mad at her for not letting me sleep over at Sandy's, though now I'm glad she didn't.

'Sit down,' Rachel whispers.

It's her game. I sit cross-legged like I always do and she throws the blanket over our heads. Then she says to lean back while she examines me, just like a doctor she explains.

'Don't be afraid.'

I lean back on my elbows and close my eyes. I feel her small fingers poking me and moving things, then touching somewhere between my legs. I jump.

'What was that?'

'Don't worry. You'll like it. It feels really good.'

The wood is rough against my bare bum and I'm afraid I might get a splinter so I don't dare move. It must be okay if Rachel does it. She touches me again, this time keeping her finger on me, moving it back and forth. I wriggle and feel hot, her finger keeps moving. It feels—strange. I close my eyes, the muscles in my tummy get hard, her finger moving, moving, moving. And suddenly—I pee all over her hand.

'MotherofGod!' she exclaims.

I jump up, yanking my panties on backwards, shorts on forwards, start toward the ladder.

'Where ya goin'?' she asks.

'I gotta go home,' I say, climbing down the first rungs.

'Don't go. Look, I'm sorry. It's a stupid game. Let's play Barbies.'

I look at the wooden rung. 'Maybe later. Mom wants me to dust my room,' I lie. 'I'll see you after lunch.'

My feet crush the brittle beige lawns, into the house, my room, my bed. I'll never play that game again. Never. Even if Rachel does play it. It's wrong. No one ever said so exactly but I know. I'm not allowed to take a bath with my brother anymore. And when I go shopping with Mom she makes me wait outside the dressing room. Not that I ever liked being in there, seeing her pink fat bulging out of her girdle and bra. Once I saw her pee in the bathroom and she had all this hair—I swear from her thighs practically to her waist. I couldn't believe it.

I don't see anything anymore. I'm too old.

When I go back to the tree house after lunch, Rachel pretends nothing has happened. She's packed Barbie and Ken's clothes in a little box—a trunk, she says—ready for a surprise trip to Florida. But Barbie doesn't want to go; she wants to save money for the wedding and to buy a house. They have a big argument, but of course they make up and go away on the trip.

It's such a hot day, even in the little tree house. After a while, Rachel and I sit on the edge of the platform dangling our legs, arms resting on the railing and watch the yard. Rosie comes out to hang some sheets on the line and sings some old song, a real sad song the way she sings it so slow and low.

> *Let us pause in life's pleasures and count its many tears,*
> *While we all sup sorrow with the poor,*
> *There's a song that will linger forever in our ears,*
> *Oh! Hard times, come again no more*

I turn away so Rachel won't see me wiping the tears from my face. Poor Rachel. I start putting away the Barbie things, sorting the little shoes back into the black plastic cosmetic bag. Oh, Rachel. 'Sup sorrow.' That's what she'll be doing when her mom dies. It's so unfair.

––––––––––

The next week school starts. Rachel goes to the Catholic school and I'm in Mrs Ketchum's grade six with dumb old Sandy who hates me now. She has a new best friend—Tina something-or-other, who just moved here from Fayetteville, North Carolina. Whenever Mrs Ketchum isn't looking, Sandy sticks her tongue out at me or crosses her eyes. She's an idiot, but I'm afraid to say anything. I don't want to make her mad—she could do something to me on the way home. I keep working and ignoring her but it's boring doing the same old stuff we did in grade five. And Mrs Ketchum makes me stand in the hallway during the Lord's Prayer and Pledge of Allegiance because I'm Canadian. I could stay in for the prayer but she says it's too disruptive, in and out, so Sammy Goldstein and I stand out in the hallway, listening to the murmur of voices up and down the corridor.

After school I race home to avoid Sandy and meet Rachel. She's not allowed to leave the yard now because of her mom. Mary doesn't have time to keep track of all of them anymore.

One day in late September, I arrive at Rachel's after school and she's furious because Mary got a little bird, a red finch, from her dad for no reason at all.

'I've been asking for a pet forever. She never even wanted a bird,' she storms. 'And it's not her birthday or anything.'

'You're like Cinderella,' I say, 'and she's the evil stepsister. But you know how that turns out!'

Rachel doesn't even giggle. I've never seen her angry. Ever.

Still she's gentle with the finch; Princess is her name. She's incredibly small and soft, her red feathers, delicate. Best of all is her song, chirpy, yet sad at the same time. She has all these bird toys—mirrors, bells—plus columns of pretty seeds to nibble at. Rachel and I linger in Mary's bedroom, watching Princess, stroking her little head, lounging on the big bed.

Then Rachel says we should try on some of Mary's clothes. 'She has the best stuff. I get hand-me-downs. Two sisters, then me. Everything's worn out.'

I think of Cinderella again. 'What if we get caught?' I ask.

'We won't. Everyone's at school or sports and stuff. Rosie's out shopping. Come on, nothing's going to happen.'

'Hey, look at these,' she says, holding out new orange-flowered flared pants and matching poor-boy shirt.

They're beautiful. I hate my dresses and skirts with the layers of scratchy petticoats and the blouses with buttons that always come undone. Most are hand-me-downs from the daughter of one of Mom's friends, a woman down the street whose husband and son were killed in Vietnam last year. Her daughter is three years older than me and won't even say hi. I don't mind. It's too weird since I'm always wearing her dresses. They're nothing like these pants and shirt. Mary is so lucky. Well, except she doesn't have any time for friends, even though she's pretty and smart. Not that it's unusual to have no friends—not for us army brats, 'D slash C: dependent/children,' as Dad calls us. Not when you move every couple years. Some kids never settle in. Like Ward. He's just making a friend and we move. Still you'd think Mary would have time for a few friends—even boys. But Rachel said their dad would kill her if she went out with a boy. I'm glad I'm not Catholic.

I want to try on the flared pants and poor-boy top, I want it so much and I hate myself for being a coward, afraid Mary might get mad at me.

'You try something on,' I say.

Rachel smiles, doesn't even call me chicken or anything. She chooses a rich blue party dress with a scooped neckline and swirling silk skirt. She takes off her school uniform blouse and blue skirt and slips it on, lets it swish down, nearly to the floor.

'Let me do up the sash,' I say, leaping from the bed.

We look in the mirror. The dress is too big in the top, but she's beautiful. There's something so pretty about the shiny fabric and deep colour against her blond curls and fair skin.

'Can I have this dance?' I ask, stooping into an awkward bow.

'Si señor,' she says, holding out her small hand. I take her in my arms like I've seen the grown-ups do at my parents' parties and we swing around the room, faster and faster, wilder and wilder, giggling and hooting.

'Stop, stop. Too fast,' she gasps. And we collapse on the bed, laughing and laughing.

Suddenly, Mary appears. 'What's this!' she shrieks. 'That's my best dress, Rachel. Get it off, NOW! I'm telling Dad.'

'You get all the best stuff,' Rachel yells. 'It's no fair. And you boss us around like you're our mom but you're not. You're not!'

She races out the door, holding the skirt above her knees.

'I'm telling Dad,' Mary calls after her. I run after my friend. It's hard to keep up, but I catch a glimpse of blue climbing the tree house ladder. She's sitting in the playhouse, crying, tears falling all over the skirt.

'Rachel,' I say, sitting down next to her. 'Don't cry.'

'It's so unfair,' she cries, pounding her fists into her lap.

'I know,' I say, helplessly.

'I hate her. I wish she was dead. She's the prettiest and Dad loves her the most. And after Mom dies no one will love me anymore. No one.'

'Oh, Rachel, don't say that. Your sisters and brothers love you. And I'm sure your Dad does too. Dads are mean and everything, but they love us.' My words sound false even to me and I think of my dad and how I wish he'd go away on a trip forever.

Rachel wipes her face on the skirt of the dress, goes over to the tree-house window and looks out across the yard, into Mary's bedroom window where the little birdcage sways gently in the breeze.

'I'm going to let it go,' Rachel whispers.

'What?'

She turns to me. 'I'm going to let the bird go.'

'You'll get caught.'

'No, I'll be careful. I'll make it seem like Mary just left its door open, then Princess can go free. It's cruel to keep a little bird in a cage anyway, don't you think?'

'I don't know. She's tame now. You know like in *Born Free*? How will she know where to get food and stuff?'

Rachel picks at a scab on her elbow. 'You think I'm mean, don't you?'

'No, no. You're mad because Mary gets all the attention.'

'I'll never be like her.' She hugs her knees to her chest, buries her head between them and begins to gently rock. I know she's crying again and I put my arm around her shoulders.

'Don't cry, Rachel, please don't cry.'

She turns to me and kisses me. On the lips. I jerk away at first but she moves in, presses again and I like it. I close my eyes, and I feel her little tongue flick against my lips, then she breaks away.

'Rub me?' she whispers.

I nod and wipe her face with my shirttail. She hikes up her dress, takes off her panties and sits cross-legged, leaning back. I had no idea it was so complicated down there. Little puffy pieces of skin to push aside, then more little parts.

'What do I touch?' I whisper.

'I dunno. Everything. Just rub it. Gently. You know, like I did for you.'

I touch her gingerly and it's soft, unbelievably soft. I stroke my finger all the way up the opening, then down, again and again.

'That's it,' she whispers. So I keep doing it. The same thing over and over until it's kind of boring but she seems to still like it, she's making soft sounds, so I don't want to stop. She closes her eyes.

I look out the little window behind her, across the yard to the street. A big black car goes by. I keep stroking Rachel. Then an ambulance pulls into their driveway.

'Look!' I say.

Rachel turns to see, but the ambulance has swung around to the front of the house where you can't see it.

'What?' asks Rachel.

I can't tell her. I can't be the one.

'Oh, nothing,' I lie. 'I thought I saw a fancy bird, but it was a dumb old sparrow.'

My stomach feels sick. How can I tell her that her mother is probably dying right now, might even be dead? My mom would know what to do, but I don't. I feel so sad—not the crying kind of sad, the aching kind, deep in my chest. I want to go home.

'I better go, Rachel. It's almost suppertime and I have to set the table.'

I stop at the top of the ladder, watching her smooth down the skirt of Mary's fancy dress. I want to say something to make everything like it was before.

'You look beautiful in that dress,' I say. 'Better than Mary ever could.'

'Do you think?' she asks.

'Oh yeah.' I hesitate, but can't think of anything else to say. 'See ya.'

I run home and sneak a long swig of Pepto-Bismol.

'UP IN THE AIR, JUNIOR BIRDMEN'

Dad slams the front door, heads into the wild blue yonder. 'Don't tell anyone,' he warns as he leaves. My normal family: mother, father, teenaged son and daughter. Names all starting with the letter *W*: Wanda and Ward, Wayne and Winifred. Military family, air force brats. Dad always says we should be glad we aren't grunts—army—who are only one step removed from the bums outside the Salvation Army on 104th Street. That's what he says.

A perfectly normal family until September 15, 1972. Six-fifteen. Supper eaten, Ward and I have washed the dishes with our usual squabbling. I've hidden two freshly chipped plates at the bottom of the stack, hoping not to catch shit, hoping at the very least to share the blame with Ward. We sit around the kitchen table under harsh fluorescent lights.

'Your mother and I have something to tell you,' says Dad.

'I have nothing to tell,' Mom mumbles, but no one pays attention.

I glance out the window to see if Janet is there yet. We're supposed to meet in the park to hang out; I want to ask her about Darcy and talk about our first week in grade nine: the new kids, who likes who, Mr T, our handsome new homeroom teacher. Janet's dad is a pilot and they live in the very nicest PMQ—the only single—in the whole bunch. Ours is a semi-detached with pink siding. But at least we aren't at Namao, the base, which is miles and miles outside town. We live in the middle of Edmonton on what used to be the base, surrounded by civilian homes, a shopping mall and the industrial airport, which is the old air force airport. I'm glad to be off-base for once, away from the dingy grey clapboard buildings, the endless rules, the gangs of kids and the twenty-four-hour clock that I always get wrong.

'This will come as a shock,' continues Dad.

Suddenly Ward lands a vicious kick below my knee. I wince and instinctively kick back, but miss. I pause, aim and fire to the left of Ward, landing a good one on his shin. I smirk.

'This is serious, Wanda,' Dad says, frowning. I recognize the edge in his voice—he'll be yelling soon if I don't watch it. I straighten up, fold my hands in my lap. Fix my eyes on the brown table. No trouble that way. I wish he'd get on with it. Janet will be waiting.

———

Where is Janet anyway? I twirl in the swing, my long, tangled hair spreading out around my head. Twirl, whirl till I'm dizzy sick. Why can't we tell anyone? Dad's such a jerk. And who would I tell anyway? Janet would blab for sure. The swing begins to unwind, spinning faster and faster. I drag my feet in the coarse sand, dirtying the toes of my new white runners.

Crappy shoes. Mom's too chintzy to buy Adidas. Or Levi's hip-huggers. I tried asking Dad. 'Do you think I'm made of money?' he bellowed, jabbing his finger in my face. I felt like biting it off. It's not fair. They spend tons. New Buick. French wine. Dinners at restaurants with real tablecloths and butter curls on beds of ice.

'I'll save my babysitting money then,' I blurted.

'Fine,' he said, 'waste your money on clothes. Just don't come crying to me when it's time for college.'

There's no pleasing him. I trace my finger around the red bruise on my leg where Ward kicked me. It's gonna be real gross: black then green then sickly yellow.

'Just wait until you have kids of your own!' Dad says. 'Just wait.'

I can't wait to leave home.

I lean back in the swing, losing myself in the blue sky, singing softly:

Up in the air, Junior Birdmen,
Up in the air, upside down
Up in the air, Junior Birdmen,
Keep your noses off the ground.

I can't remember learning the song—I've always known it. I sort of remember Dad singing it, too, but that can't be.

I pull a pack of sunflower seeds from my jeans pocket and suck on a salty shell. I carefully crack it lengthwise with my teeth, easing the seed out with my tongue and spitting the shell into the dust.

———

'Your mother and I have decided ...'

'I haven't decided anything,' Mom interrupts again. 'This is your doing.'

Dad sighs. I look up, surprised—for once he's biting his tongue. Something *is* wrong.

'I'm sorry to say this'—he pauses—'but your mother and I are separating. We're getting a divorce.'

The room collapses in silence. The traffic outside stops. Slowly, the sound of rushing water fills my head. I strain to hear him.

'I'm on tour in Germany for a month and I'll be moving out after that.'

'Where?' Ward whispers.

'Toronto.'

Like waves now, the rushing recedes with each heartbeat.

'You might as well know it all. I've met a woman, a friend of a friend. I didn't mean for this to happen.' He pauses again. 'We're getting married as soon as we can.'

His tone is quiet yet firm. Polite. Like I imagine he talks to the ground crew. Mom stares at her hands, clenched white on top of the table.

'This is very difficult for me. It doesn't mean I don't love you kids ...'

But ... The word lingers in the air like smoke from damp firewood. Acrid. Making the eyes sting. *But.* We all hear it.

A motorcycle screams down the street. The waves in my ears break in a crescendo. His voice booms across the table. 'You'll stay with your mother of course. I know Toronto's a long way off, but I'll arrange for you to visit Francine and me. And I'll come here too.'

Francine. Fran-cine, Plasti-cine, like a machine.

Ward glances up. Our eyes meet then dart away.

'Any questions?' Dad demands, like it's a briefing before a mission.

I push a strand of hair behind my ear, covertly brushing aside a tear, but I sniff anyway. Sniffling. Blubbering, Dad calls it. 'Stop your blubbering or I'll give you something to cry about,' is a standard-issue threat, followed closely by 'There's more where that came from.'

'Don't worry,' Dad says, 'everything will work out all right for you. Your mother and I will make sure of that.'

'Oh,' he says, 'one more thing. Don't tell anyone. It's going to be difficult enough without a lot of gossip and lies floating around the neighbourhood.'

I stare at the tabletop. Don't tell anyone — the words fill my head. Pretend everything is fine. Nice family of four, names all starting with *W*, new car, snow blower and stereo console — still fine, doing fine. Pretend there's no problem.

A transport truck roars by on 118th Avenue.

I scrape my chair across the floor, watch Dad cringe.

'Can I go to the park?'

'May I,' he retorts automatically.

'May I go to the park?'

'Be home by nine,' Mom says in a flat voice.

Home by nine. Everyone else gets to stay out till nine-thirty, ten even. In summer it's too light to sleep anyway; you might as well stay up. Two evenings after we moved here, I went out to play and Mom said to be home by dark. But it was July and it was light out until eleven. I played swing tag with a group of girls — mostly the daughters of grunts, but I didn't care. I was determined to be popular this time. Mom was pissed — 'We were so worried about you, young lady' — and made me stay in the next day and hem curtains. I probably would've had to stay in and help anyway. Now it doesn't pay to break curfew. You never know what the punishment will be: a few days grounded or a whole week—it depends on their mood. And it's so boring staying at home, doing chores for Mom. Endless polishing: Hawes Lemon Oil on furniture, Silvo on flatware, Brasso on copper pots. Last Friday, I finally got the nerve to ask Dad if I could stay out later.

'Show me that I can trust you, that you'll be home on time,' Dad said. 'Then we'll consider a later curfew.'

I looked at my shoes. Yeah, right. In a million years. He'll never trust me. Questions me over every little thing. Always assumes I'm lying.

————————

I pop another sunflower seed in my mouth. Betcha she's pretty, Francine. Petite. Me and mom, we're big-boned—not like those old Ukrainian ladies going to the church on 118th—but with wide hips. I'm 39 inches already. And small breasted. I pull up the strap on my training bra. My tongue is numb from salt. I push the ten-cent pack of seeds back into my jeans pocket. Janet is 36C already. She probably is too, a 36C. Fran-seen from Paree. Fancy Francey.

> Francey, Francey,
> Puddin' and pie,
> Kissed my dad,
> And made me cry.

None of my friends' parents are divorced. Except Steve's and he's a reject. Janet says his dad's in jail. And his family lives in a shack. Maybe we will too. Mom makes diddly-squat at that stupid accounting office. Sitting there all day, spazzy-looking earphones in, typing. At home she plunges her finger in her ear, vibrates, dredges up the waxy bits—bad as picking your nose in public. If she took better care of herself maybe ...

'Wanda, Wanda!' Janet waves wildly from across the playground, her breasts bouncing under her T-shirt. 'Hey! Come here.'

I sprint off the swing, dash across the yard. Stalks of weeds scratch my bare ankles; a scabby mosquito bite bleeds again.

'Darcy's hitting a tennis ball against the gym wall,' Janet says.

'He is?' I say. 'Let's go by, okay? Like we're going somewhere else.'

Mom says I'm boy crazy. 'You'll get a reputation,' she warns. 'Wait for them to phone you.' She's so old-fashioned. This is the '70s—girls can do the phoning.

I stop walking. 'Do I look okay?'

'Got a comb?' Janet asks.

'No.'

'You're fine.'

We turn the corner and there he is, wearing his new purple back-to-school shirt.

'Hiya, Darcy,' I say.

'Hi, Wanda,' he says. 'Hey, Janet,' he says, giving a small wave.

What a hunk!

'How do you like our homeroom teacher?' I ask.

'He's okay, I guess.' There is a small pause. 'Have you guys heard the new Yes album?'

'Parts,' I lie. 'It's far out.'

'I got it today. Wanna come over and listen?'

'Sure,' I say, and my heart races like I've just finished the four-hundred-yard dash. 'You want to, Janet?' and I raise my eyebrows meaningfully—meaning Janet should let me go alone—but she doesn't seem to notice.

'Yeah, sure,' Janet says. 'My sister has that album. I love it.'

Janet and Darcy talk about it all the way to his PMQ. I lag behind, wondering how people can talk so much about music. Blab, blab, blab. At least I won't have to listen to Dad blabbing anymore. He's always blabbing, criticizing.

'You kids can do your share around here, too; this isn't a free ride. We're going to put up the storm windows. I don't care if it takes all day. Wanda, you'll clean them. And do a good job, or you'll be doing them over again till you do.' And inevitably later on, yelling, 'Can't you do anything right? An eight-year-old could do a better job!'

I'm so tired of the endless badgering. He's getting worse here in Edmonton. Maybe it's because his job is so crummy. He hasn't been promoted for a long time and now he's navigating on the Buffalo—not even the Hercules, which is at least bigger. They're both a far cry from the 747 he used to work on. Transporting boxes now, instead of VIPs. Maybe he's been blacklisted as a womanizer, a liar, doomed to horrible jobs.

I couldn't care less if he leaves us. It'll be better without him.

My feet are freezing on the concrete floor. I fling a black sock into the washing machine with Dad's pale green uniform shirts. They all wear green now, ever since Trudeau's unification. The more Dad rails against Trudeau, the more I love him. I collect photos of him, hide them in my bottom drawer. Dad wears air force plaid ties whenever he's in civvies.

'Trudeau has no concept of the military mentality,' he booms. 'It's nothing but politics and the pretense of saving a few bucks. There will always be a separate army, navy and air force. Always.'

I add too much soap to the laundry and use the hottest water setting, hoping the black socks will ruin the shirts.

> *There was an old man who could fly,*
> *Who made all the women sigh. . . .*

He wouldn't let me babysit tonight. I'll never save enough for Levi's. Friday night and I have to stay in because it's his last night. Big hairy deal.

> *There was a man who could yell,*
> *He screamed: 'You can all go to hell!'*
> *I'm leaving today,*
> *No matter what you say,*
> *That selfish man who could yell.*

'Wanda!' Dad calls from upstairs.

'Yeah?'

'Don't bellow,' he hollers. 'Come when you're called.'

I bang upstairs. He's sitting at the kitchen table, papers, chequebook spread out in front of him.

'Sit down,' he says, indicating a chair with his pen.

I slouch, head hung.

'Sit up straight, Wanda. That's not an attractive posture.'

I straighten up and stare at the vinyl wallpaper: dancing blue and green teakettles. How stupid can you get?

He snaps his chequebook closed and places his pen precisely on top.

'Your mother is worried that she won't be able to handle you while I'm gone. She's got a lot on her plate right now.'

'Uh-huh,' I mutter. I avoid his eyes, those eyes that mirror my own, the left slightly squinty, shifty.

'I want you to promise to be good while I'm gone,' he says.

Be good. Be good like I'm a two-year-old kid in Woodward's department store?

'I'll try.'

'You'll have to do more than bloody try,' he says, voice rising, finger poised. 'We're a family, we have to stick together during this. Help each other.'

'You're not sticking with us,' I yell, shocking myself. I instinctively brace myself for a smack upside the head. But he sighs heavily, spreads his hands in front of him, examines his meticulously filed nails.

'We've been through this,' he says. 'I'm doing my best. Maybe you'll understand when you get older.'

I say nothing.

'You can go now,' he says.

Dismissed. I loiter on the basement stairs. What happens now? Will we have to move? Again? Every three or four years, another school. No friends. I should've asked. It is military housing, after all. Can't stay in a PMQ after your father's left the family. Left us wondering.

At five-thirty in the morning we all get up to say goodbye. Mom has a red stripe across her forehead where she's just removed the tape that held her bangs down. They shared a bed last night; I heard them coming out of the bedroom. How could she after what he's done? I shiver and tighten the belt on my dressing gown. I have such a bad stomachache. I really need a slug of Pepto-Bismol.

Dad phones a taxi and we wait. Mom rinses the coffee percolator, bangs the grinds into the garbage can. He tidies papers in his brief-case—the one Mom gave him last Christmas. Expensive leather. Ward stares out the black window. I slouch on a chair, fold and refold the cloth belt of my dressing gown.

The taxi's headlights illuminate the teakettles on the wallpaper. Dad snaps his briefcase shut and dives into his overcoat.

'You two be good for your mother,' he says, eyeing me. He kisses Mom on the cheek. A wall of cold air engulfs us. He slams the door, heads into the wild blue yonder. Bastard. I leave Mom peering out the frosted window.

——————

I wake, sweating. Ever since Dad left, Mom keeps the furnace blasting. I kick off the covers, turn on my reading light: 3:23 a.m. I collapse on my pillow. What a dream! Sort of a dream, but real too—like a memory.

I'm about six years old and I wake up in the middle of the night to Mom shouting: 'How can you do this to us?' The hall light flicks on and Mom races by the door in her pale yellow negligee with the daisy trim. Dad lumbers after her, thump, thump, thump. Peeking under my lashes, I see him pausing to close my door. I get out of bed and open the door a crack, peering down the hall: Mom stands outside on the porch, arms wrapped around her crying: 'You're leaving me out in the cold. You're leaving your whole family out in the cold.'

'Come on, dear. Come back to bed. We'll sort this out.'

More words, quieter and they go into the kitchen. I hear the splash of water in the metal kettle. I want to spy on them but I'm afraid of being caught and punished. I jump back in bed, pull the sheets over my head.

Did it happen? It seems so real. Did he try to leave when I was six? I pound my pillow. Why did Mom put up with it? I think of Mom crying on the porch. Crying and pleading with Dad. And then I remember: she slept with him the night before he left us. I feel overwhelmed with shame. She's so weak, so dependent on him for everything. I switch the light off, lie in the darkness, staring at the dark ceiling. A car squeals around the corner. I tense, wait for the crash.

———————

I tell my mother we're going bowling. She gives me a long, cool stare. Obviously, she doesn't believe me.

'Bowling,' I repeat.

Darcy's mother is at his aunt's for the night and he's having a party. No one asks about fathers; they're always away on exercise or courses or something. Darcy's older sister bought beer for him. He says he drinks all the time.

'You can't go out in that top,' Mom says.

The red-and-white crop top exposes my midriff, my belly button. I was saving for Levi's but then I saw the top at Woodward's.

'But Mom, all the girls wear them. I've been wearing it to school.'

'It isn't decent, and it's too cold outside. If you want to go out, change.'

Right. I thump up the stairs. What does Mom know? She looks ridiculous in her too-young hot pants outfit that shows her varicose veins. Or the peasant-style dresses, cut too low for an office, with tight belts that make her stomach bulge out. And she wears that mangy wig Thursdays and Fridays because her hair's a mess and she doesn't go to the hairdresser till Saturday. At home, she's always chilly and drapes a shapeless beige cardigan over her shoulders. She used to dress so nicely when I was little.

I grab my blue T-shirt. Janet and I each bought one last summer, matching T-shirts with a huge butterfly across the chest. When Dad saw Janet's shirt he said, 'Your butterfly has sure spread its wings!' Janet blushed and giggled; I was so grossed out.

'That's better,' Mom says. 'You look nice.'

I shrug.

'You should say "thank you". Don't be afraid of accepting a compliment, Wanda.'

'Thanks, Mom.' I give her a half smile, feeling guilty for thinking such mean things about her.

Janet isn't ready yet, even though I spent half an hour getting the stupid knots out of my hair and was sure I'd be late. I watch her carefully draw a blue line under each eye, then smooth light blue powder on her lids.

'Want some?' she asks.

'Maybe a bit, just so it's natural. I don't think Darcy likes a lot.'

'Stay still,' says Janet and begins lining my eyes.

'Who taught you?' I ask.

'My sister. It's fun.'

'Nicole's so lucky. Her hair is gorgeous.'

'Yeah, and she has like a million guys phoning.'

We both silently consider the limitless possibilities of popularity.

'Do you think she's done it?' I ask. 'You know …'

'Wanda!' says Janet. 'No way! We're waiting till we're married. Mom says "Why buy the cow if you can get the cream for free?" '

I say nothing. I've always imagined the before—the dates and kisses, hand-holding and hugs, going around with someone, attention, gifts —but what about after, going all the way?

We clamber down Darcy's basement steps in our stocking feet to the dimly lit rec room. A lone red light shines in a corner and a black-light poster of Led Zeppelin glows on the far wall.

Of course we're the first. Too eager. He'll know I like him. I'm such a spazz.

'Wanna beer?' he asks.

'Sure,' I say, casual-like, as if I drink all the time. Ward always pours Dad's beers and drinks the bit left in the bottom of the bottle. Dad says ladies don't drink beer. Mom nearly always drinks rye and Coke, though sometimes, on really hot summer days, she'll have a shandy: half beer, half ginger ale.

Darcy hands me a bottle of Lethbridge Pil; our fingers connect and a surge of warmth charges me.

'Wanna glass?' he asks.

'No thanks,' I say, but then Janet takes a glass so maybe if ladies do drink beer, they take a glass. Who cares? I chug half the bottle so I won't have to taste it. It's horrible. Bitter.

People arrive. Bruce and John, but I immediately forget who's who. Leanne's wearing a new white bubble top and flared green jeans. She always has the coolest clothes. I sit on the edge of the couch sipping the dregs of my beer.

'You just take a pop bottle and put a bearing inside. Shake it and it breaks a hole in the bottom. It makes a perfect hookah,' one of the high school boys is saying.

'Everyone has one at Tech,' says the other.

Churchill Technical High School. Parties, boys, hookahs and who knows. I can't wait. Leanne comes and sits beside me.

'Did you hear about Sonia?' she whispers.

'I heard she's pregnant.'

'Yeah, but it's worse—you can't tell anyone—but she told me her father is the one, you know, the one . . .'

'No way! Her father? No way!'

One of the boys glances in our direction.

'Shh,' Leanne hisses in my ear.

'Wilkinson's the best quarterback ever. They would never trade him,' says one of the boys.

'She's gone,' whispers Leanne. 'Went to her gran's in Calgary.'

'She must be lying about her father. I mean how . . .?'

Leanne shrugs. 'Sonia says her parents are getting a divorce. I gotta go to the can. Talk to ya later.'

Why is the most popular girl in school telling me secrets? Is it because of Darcy? Am I part of some in-crowd now?

'Want another beer?' Darcy asks.

'Sure. Thanks.'

He hands me a bottle and sits beside me. Puts his arm around my shoulders. My armpits are instantly soaked. I can't believe he's doing this. He actually likes me. We're about the same height so I slouch down a bit. He leans over and kisses me, slightly off-centre. I pull him to me and kiss him back. He slips his tongue between my teeth, probing my mouth and pressing my lips harder. I feel a familiar swelling between my legs, the feeling I get when I touch myself. Not that I do that anymore. It feels pathetic, like admitting I can't find a boyfriend.

The music stops and Darcy pulls away abruptly, wipes his mouth with the back of his hand and goes to the turntable.

'Wanda, what are you doing?' whispers Janet. 'Everyone's staring.'

I take a long swig of beer. 'I don't care!'

I go and crouch beside Darcy, begin flipping through the albums propped against the wall, searching for one I know. Everyone else is so much more with it.

'Do you like this?' Darcy asks, holding up the Beatles, *Abbey Road*.

'I love it,' I say, relieved at the sight of the familiar cover.

'Something' comes over the speakers. 'Wanna dance?' Darcy asks. I nod and smile. He puts his arms around me and brings me close. He smells like sun, sweat, beer. Please don't let me stink, I pray. Please. He tightens his arms and I feel hardness between his legs. I close my eyes, but the room reels and my stomach churns, so I pop them open, wish he would stop twirling so quickly. I kiss him to stop him from moving, keep my eyes open. The song ends and I step away quickly. He grabs me around my waist. 'Wanna see my room?' he whispers.

I nod.

He takes me by the hand, takes me through a door I hadn't noticed before. The door closes, the music fades. It's dark except for a pulsating lava lamp. He leads me to the double bed. I perch on the edge.

'Cool room,' I say, 'I like—'

He puts one finger under my chin, turns my face toward him. He's done this before—he's been with girls before. Here. He kisses me, slides his tongue into my mouth: I taste fresh, cool beer, feel tongue caressing tongue. I lean into him, pushing, wanting. Then he slips his hand under my top. My training bra! Oh my God, I could die. But he moves deftly under the bra and grabs my breast, hard. I wince. He moves to the other and squeezes it.

'You're just starting, eh?' he murmurs. I blush, face on fire. He plunges his tongue into my ear. A mucky wet sound like when Mom's kneading ingredients for meat loaf. It makes my head ring. He twists my breast ...

'Darcy, please don't.' But he keeps on and I jerk my head away—leaving his tongue dangling—and pull his hand out of my top. But he moves it between my legs, rubbing the crotch of my jeans.

'Stop, stop that. It hurts,' I say, pushing him away.

'Just relax,' he says. And in one fluid movement he unzips my jeans and pushes his hand under my cotton underwear, plunging down. He comes at me, eyes closed, mouth gaping.

I turn aside so he gets a mouthful of hair and yank his hand out of my pants. 'Stop it NOW!' My voice rising in a frightened crescendo.

He clutches my upper thigh, pinching. 'Why'd you come? I know you want it. You've been after me for months, hanging around the house.'

My chest collapses. 'Not like this, Darcy,' I whisper. 'Everyone will know,' I add meekly, nodding toward the door.

'You're a tease,' he snarls. 'A tease and a boobless baby. I was just being nice to you.'

I zip my jeans, bolt through the door and grab Janet's hand. 'We have to leave!' I whisper.

'What happened?' Janet calls, the sound echoing against the silent houses. I keep walking as fast as I can.

'Wait up, eh,' Janet says.

I stop in the semi-darkness of our back alley, my heart pounding, beer seething in my stomach.

'Wanda?'

'I thought it would be special, I thought he liked me,' I say, raging against tears. 'Mom was right'—there's a catch in my voice—'I should play hard to get.'

'What did he say?'

'He really queered me out. He knew I'd been hanging around the house, watching him and then he goes, like, I want it—I want IT!—he grabs me, feels me up and he wouldn't stop.'

'He's a pig,' Janet spits out. 'Are you okay? Did he hurt you?'

'I'm okay now.' Tears slip down my cheeks. 'He called me a tease, a baby, and I left.'

'The dink, what'd he expect—you hardly know him. He's never even asked you out.'

'He never will now.'

'Who cares? You don't want a guy like that. You can do a lot better.'

'Maybe.'

'For sure, you're cute, and smart. A lot smarter than him.'

I blush in the darkness, feel warm and grateful, ashamed that I was ever jealous of Janet. We walk together down the back alley.

'What time is it?' I ask.

'Quarter to ten.'

'Frig, I'm late.' I begin running down the sidewalk then stop. 'Janet, you gotta come with me. Please. Tell Mom we lost track of time. Remember: the bowling alley. Same people, but the bowling alley.'

'Okay, sure.'

'And please don't tell anyone about Darcy,' I call over my shoulder.

'You know I won't,' Janet says between deep breaths.

The back door is closed. Funny, Mom is usually up, waiting. Watching through the screen door even if I'm a second late. I rummage for the key in the clothes-peg basket and let myself in. The kitchen is empty. I peer into the pass-through and see Mom lying on the couch, asleep.

'That's strange,' I whisper to Janet.

Janet eases the door open again. 'See ya,' she mouths.

I tiptoe upstairs, avoiding the creak on the third and sixth steps. I've done it often enough, the midnight forays to the fridge trying to settle my stomach, eating maraschino cherries out of a sticky jar or going straight for a slug of Pepto-Bismol. I throw my clothes on the floor, yank on my faded flannel nightgown, don't bother brushing my teeth.

I lie down and close my eyes, but my head whirls. I feel like I'm gonna puke. I sit up, cradle my head in my hands. Darcy will tell about the training bra, for sure. Ward says he talks to his friends. Brags. They'll all know I'm flat as a board. And he might say I'm a tease too, a cock tease. Oh God, oh God, no one will ever go out with me, what will I do? Why did I run away? I should have talked to the dink, said later or something, put him off. I'm such an idiot.

I turn on my reading light, illuminating its pink frilly shade that matches my bedspread. I hate pink. I lie down again, one foot over the side of the bed, planted on the pink shag carpet, eyes wide open. They'll hate me, all of them. I'm such a spazz. I'll never get a date. Never. No, no … I chew my index finger, remembering the morning Dad left and the pink stripe across Mom's forehead as she looked out the window.

Shards of the morning sun glare between the crack in the curtains, piercing my head. My brain throbs behind my left eye. My first hangover. Dad always gulped Eno after a long night at the mess—I wonder if it helps? I stumble out of bed, notice that my clothes are folded neatly on the chair. Mom. At least she didn't spend all night on the couch.

I want an aspirin but I'll have to ask Mom. All the drugs are kept in a locked box, ever since that time when I was seven and ate all the Ex-Lax. The cramps hurt so much and I didn't quite make it to the bathroom. They put a tube down my throat and pumped my stomach at the hospital. My parents' party was ruined but for once I didn't get into trouble.

I'm sitting at the kitchen table, nibbling on a piece of dry toast, when Mom comes into the kitchen, hugging her shapeless cardigan around her.

'How was bowling?' she asks.

'Great,' I say, in the same falsely cheerful tone she uses for company.

'I called the alley,' she says coolly. 'They were completely booked with a tournament.

My heart lurches, my head bangs. I can't believe she phoned! I'll be grounded until I'm eighteen. I quickly take a bite of toast.

'Where did you go?' asks Mom.

I chew intently, each chew like a stab to my brain. I blink to keep the tears dammed, swallow and say the first thing that comes into my head: 'We went to the park.'

'That doesn't make sense, Wanda.' Mom sits down across from me. 'Why would you lie about bowling so you could go to the park? You go there all the time.' Her voice rises like notes on a scale. 'Don't you dare lie to me!'

My head roars. There's no way out. I inhale slowly and breathe out. 'We went over to Darcy's, you know he's in my class. He had a few kids over. That's all. But I knew you wouldn't let me go. You never let me go anywhere.'

'And you wonder why, when you make up this elaborate story about bowling and everything. How could you, Wanda? Isn't it enough that your father lied to us?' Her voice breaks. Is that a tear slipping down her nose? My reply lumps in my throat. I'm such a spazz. After what Dad did to her. What Darcy did to me is nothing compared with that.

'I'm sorry, Mom, please,' I plead. 'I wasn't thinking. I'm really sorry. I won't lie to you again. I promise. Cross my heart.'

Mom pulls a Kleenex out of the cuff of her cardigan and dabs at her eyes. 'Can't you imagine what it's like for me? Him away half the time and me never knowing ...' She pauses, and slows her pace. 'Never knowing when the flirting would change and some woman would go after him. Women were always attracted to your father. So I worried and wondered every time he went away. And here it's happened again.'

Again. I hang on to the word. Of course. I was right—it wasn't a dream, it was a memory.

'I need some peace. It's hard enough without you lying, too.'

I nod, stare at my red and bitten index finger. She was good to Dad, but he didn't appreciate her. He's a bastard.

I hear the little girl next door shouting: 'Liar, liar, pants on fire.'

DO YOU THINK SHE KNOWS?

Hot, stale air shoots into the car. After whirring madly all day, the heater in my rust-pocked Toyota is now stuck on full-blast. I bang the dash, fiddle with the levers and finally open the window a crack. An icy gust swirls into the car, envelops my face as I squint at the modest bungalow across the street. A few moments ago the driveway was bare, pure, black edged with neat curbs of snow. Now the asphalt is white. Snow twists through the air, disappearing upward.

Glancing in the rear-view mirror, I can barely make out the cars of the two other reporters. We are all waiting for Josef Donajski to get home, but I'm the only one who knows him. He's a founding member of the thirty-year-old Madawan Horticultural Society. I've written notices for *The Madawan Post* about his seminars on exotic bulb sources and cutting propagation. Until recently, he was just this old man with a foreign accent.

I find it hard to believe this is happening in my town. I think of Madawan as *my* town when I'm talking to outsiders, like these two reporters from the city dailies. Then I'm the one who knows about the mayor's racist tendencies, the local pyromaniac's latest brush fire, the town's waning prosperity. I find myself speaking with the local twang, the exaggerated, prolonged *a*'s—'baaag', 'gaaag'—and using the local expressions like 'He only has one oar in the water,' or saying 'Old Year's Evening' instead of New Year's Eve.

But in the end I'm as much an outsider as these reporters. Even after five years at *The Post* people still ask where I'm from and I still say Ottawa because it's close and familiar, easier than running through the litany of the dozen or so places from my itinerant childhood. And they invariably reply, 'Oh, so you're not from the Valley.' As if that explains *everything*. I know they've drawn a line: you versus us.

It might be different if I married someone local. Someone like Ron.

Snow flies through the open window, melting against my face. I brush it away with my hand, roughly run my fingers through my hair, then roll up the window tightly.

Last September, Donajski asked Ron to represent him. Ron gave him the name of another lawyer in the city, someone with experience in international law. He phoned to tell me about it.

'After he left, the new secretary came in and asked who he was,' Ron added. 'She said he gave her the willies.'

Ron didn't say how the man made him feel, but then he wouldn't. He could barely choke out the words to express how he felt about me. He whispered it softly into my hair when I was half-asleep. Maybe he was hoping I was fully asleep. 'I love you,' he murmured to the dark.

'You shouldn't be telling me about Donajski,' I said to Ron. 'You're not supposed to tell me about your clients. It's unethical.' And I hung up on him.

He wooed me back with a graceful spray of deep pink saponaria backed by towering, shell-like eustoma—mid-summer splendours on a chilling late-autumn day. But he didn't apologize or admit he was wrong. The card was signed by the florist: Love, Ron.

Five-twelve and it's dark already. I feel for my camera on the seat beside me, make sure the flash is securely attached. The bungalow's porch light flicks on, illuminating the falling snow. Donajski's wife is home waiting for him. He's late. She must be losing it, 'flipping her wig,' as they say around here.

The neighbours seem to pity her. Ron's cousin, who lives next door to the Donajskis, said she hardly ever sees 'the wife'—that's how everyone says it around here. Not Joanne or Susan, just 'the wife,' like the butcher, or the mailman: someone filling a role.

'I don't think her English is that good,' the cousin said, then hesitated. 'But she's polite, ya know. Always says gidday. Smiles.'

Other neighbours said Donajski takes her to buy groceries every Wednesday, waits in the car while she shops. And she works in the yard, raking grass, then dead leaves; shovelling dirt, then snow. I couldn't find anyone who has ever had a conversation with her. An odd thing in Madawan where everyone talks too much, knows too much about their neighbours. No one even knows her first name. She is anonymous, poised on the periphery.

I fiddle with my camera, press the battery check and shoot off the flash in the dark car, illuminating empty Styrofoam cups, bits of gravel, a shard of ice. I hope to hell Anita got the photo of Donajski at the courthouse; we need one for the front page. We have an overexposed one on file: him posing with the five-pound potato he grew in his garden. People are always wandering into the office with their freaks of nature—malformed carrots that vaguely resemble Charles de Gaulle, quadruplet radishes joined at the stem, monstrous pumpkins or tomatoes. Despite the poor exposure there is something unsettling about the picture of Donajski. He stands holding his potato, back against the bare wall, looking into the camera. It's like a surreal police mug shot. I wonder if his wife clipped the newspaper photo and put it on the fridge with a magnet.

During last Sunday's stint in the darkroom, I asked Anita what she thought of Donajski's wife.

'She's an odd one all right. Never leaves the house. Has no friends,' said Anita, pressing the enlarger button, exposing a negative. 'But who knows what kind of hell she's from? He brought her over here from the old country—somewhere in Eastern Europe. She's probably grateful, you know, for the house and that. Clothes, proper food. A little comfort.'

I switched off the safety light, cracked open a canister of film and wound it in the cold metal reel.

'Do you think she knows?' I asked in the darkness. 'Do you think she knows whether he did it or not?'

'No way,' said Anita.

I remember seeing Donajski at the farmers' market, hands deep in his pockets, standing in front of dripping pails of red and orange hollyhocks, white lilies. A low card table to one side spilled over with scarlet tomatoes, potent onions and dusky cucumbers. I touched his fingers when I bought his tomatoes. They were calloused but well scrubbed, no dirt hiding in the crevices.

I shake my head in a stupor; the heat in the car is unbearable. I switch off the ignition and open the window a crack; it creaks in protest.

Maybe he's innocent. Maybe they have the wrong man. Half a century is a long time.

Donajski is accused of murdering 390 Jews in a German concentration camp in occupied Poland.

I close my eyes. Newsreel images of Auschwitz come to me, photos of starving men, living skeletons lying on bunk beds, of operating tables with drainage holes and huge vats underneath to catch the blood. My journalism profs would say it's a once-in-a-lifetime story but it makes me feel sick.

Car lights flash across my face, jerking me out of my stupor. I'm tired, so tired. A dark sedan with tinted windows drives slowly by. Maybe it's them—Donajski and his lawyer. They've probably spotted us and gone on. Maybe to the lawyer's office.

The reporter from *The Ottawa Mercury* walks toward my car. I unroll the window but he hops in the passenger side, a wall of cold air accompanying him.

'Do you think that was him?' he asks.

'Could be,' I say. 'Court got out more than an hour ago.'

'Where else would he go?' he asks.

I shrug. As if I'd tell him.

Now the reporter from *The Ottawa Dispatch* comes over. I unroll my window completely. He asks the same questions. I notice traces of icing sugar on his cheek.

'Do you think he did it?' asks the reporter from *The Dispatch*.

'No,' I say, without hesitating, then immediately wonder why I'm defending him. 'Innocent until proven guilty,' I add.

'I think he did,' says *The Mercury* reporter. 'There's too much evidence. They have witnesses.'

The other reporter nods knowingly. 'This is the perfect hideout,' he says. 'A little hick town in the middle of nowhere. No one would ever suspect. And the gardening is a nice touch.'

Jerks! I watch them waddle back to their cars. What could they possibly know?

I shiver, close the window and start the car again, cringing under the torrid blast of air, my eyes drying instantly. I flick on the wipers, cutting a swath through the snow. Across the street, a light goes on in the living room, shines through the part in the drapes. I sigh and peer at the snow whirling around the ordinary bungalow. What does Mrs Donajski know? How much does she know?

'It was like he had two lives,' I told Ron last night. 'No one had a clue about what happened before. He was just a guy selling tomatoes.'

Ron looked up from his file. 'You never know what to expect with people,' he said.

'What do you mean?'

He closed the file. 'The other day, a businessman comes in—a guy I've known since I was a kid, respected, former chair of the Chamber of Commerce. Turns out his wife caught him in bed with her best friend. Her best friend! Someone she's known for twenty-five years. And they'd been having an affair for the last ten.'

There was a pause between us. Ron raised his paper again, hiding his face.

'It's a ridiculous comparison,' I said. 'Lying about having an affair with your wife's best friend is revolting, but hardly comparable to allegedly murdering nearly four hundred people.'

'Of course,' said Ron. 'I'm only pointing out that both men are experts at deception, at hiding a part of themselves from their wives and the community. You never know with people. You think you do but you don't.'

'Then how can you trust anyone?' I asked.

'Do you want to go to Rosa's for dinner?' he asked.

After these dinners out, we visit his friends—his childhood buddies. I can't imagine keeping friends for twenty years. Anita's my oldest pal, though I've had hundreds over the years. Hundreds scattered across North America. Friends whose ardent promises at going-away parties prompted a deluge of letters that gradually dwindled to a trickle, then Christmas and birthday greetings. Then nothing. A memory and a school picture in a dusty box under my bed, packed and ready to move.

I listen carefully to the stories Ron and his friends tell. Stories about past misdemeanours and adventures that they repeat again and again after a few brews, when they are firmly in their cups. I've memorized details, the chronological order of their lives; sometimes I almost feel like I was there.

Ron has mentioned living together in his house, the house his mother grew up in. He said my Lalique vase would look perfect on his mantel. It's my prize possession, so graceful and ephemeral, my legacy from Granny C. It's held pride of place in the dozen or so apartments I've lived in since leaving my parents' house, yet I struggle to imagine it on his mantel, struggle to envision his house as my home.

Sweat trickles from my armpits, into my bra. I unbutton my coat completely and yank my scarf away from my neck. I peer at my wristwatch: 5:43. Where the hell is Donajski?

I long to be in my apartment, cooking a cheese omelette and listening to the CBC. I've managed to stay in the same place two years now—a record for me. Though I've stashed a stack of folded boxes in the back of my closet, ready to be reassembled and packed. And when I'm tired or lonely, I still find myself looking through the want ads for another apartment, drawing circles with a chewed red pencil. But that's as far as it has gone. I tried explaining it to Ron.

'I got used to moving all the time. It seemed like an easy way out,' I said. 'I kept thinking that if I moved, things would get better.'

'You were young,' Ron said. 'Adventurous. That's all.'

He refuses to believe there is anything more to it. He doesn't want to talk about anything so uncomfortable, so weird. I want him to think I'm normal, but if it were the other way around, if he had a history of moving every six months or so, I would be concerned. I would ask about it. What kind of partner wouldn't show more interest?

I think of the long evenings spent sitting on his bachelor-beige couch, talking, and it occurs to me how one-sided these conversations are. I ask question after question; he's a difficult interview. There are prolonged pauses after my questions and then truncated answers. I hear him whispering 'I love you' into the night but I have never said anything in return.

I shift my body, move my head to one side so the blast of heat jets past me. The dull roar of the engine, the whirring of the heater, the heat itself, lulls me.

It could be so pleasant, I think, closing my eyes. Ron's beautiful old house amidst the lumber baron mansions, surrounded by elegant landscaping. It's so easy to be with his old friends. His life is a sure thing. Comfortable.

Me and Mrs Donajski. Marrying into a sure thing. But now, now, look where she is, trying to believe he's innocent. Otherwise how can she stay and what would she do? What would I do if I were her ... if I were waiting for him to come home from the hearing, in through the back door, stomping loudly, dirty snow flying from his black galoshes? He sits heavily in his chair, stares at his thick fingers, the scar on his thumb where he nicked it with the pruning shears late last summer. I set a bowl of soup in front of him. Nourishing soup that has been simmering all day, first the bone boiling, steaming liquid trapping the marrow's goodness, then chunks of beef from last Sunday's roast and home-grown vegetables retrieved from the root cellar: carrots, turnips, potatoes. I set a bowl down in front of him like I have a thousand times before and he grunts in—in what? Appreciation? Acknowledgement? Disgust?

'You have to tell me,' I blurt out.

He glares and his face transforms, he becomes Ron. Ron sitting at his oak dining room table. He says, 'You never know with people. You think you do but you don't.'

I struggle to wake, then succumb again to the hot air, the engine droning.

I am outside the house, barefoot, struggling against the wind. Snow pelts my face yet I'm sweating. The wind wails in my ears, I lean into it and wade through the drifts to the front door. I tap on the window. Wait. Tap again. I peep through the glass and glimpse a small woman, Dona-jski's wife. She has huge rollers crowning her head. They look like the small orange juice tins I used to roll my own hair in in a futile attempt to control the curls. Oddly enough, the rollers perched up there make Mrs Donajski look like a middle-aged Statue of Liberty. Suddenly, she is right in front of me, her face blotchy, her red-rimmed eyes looking into mine.

'Please, Mrs Donajski ...' I begin, but she puts her finger to her lips—the universal sign for silence—then pulls the shade down between us.

A knock on the window. More knocking. Then I hear far away someone calling, 'Hey, hey in there!'

Then I'm coughing, gasping in the piercing fresh air and a man asks, 'Hey, are you all right?'

My eyelids flutter open—the reporter from *The Dispatch* reaches across my lap and turns off the motor.

'You should keep your window open in this old heap,' he says.

I struggle to catch my breath, wheezing.

'I think you got a touch of carbon monoxide poisoning,' he says. 'Let me drive you to the hospital.'

'No,' I gasp. 'No, I'm fine.'

He tells me to breathe deeply, pats my back. I sip the cold air tentatively.

'You really don't look so good. Let me drive you in.'

'No, no really,' I whisper, embarrassed to be seen like this. I clear my throat, take a gulp of air. 'I'm feeling better already. It's okay.'

'Well, if you're sure,' says the reporter, pausing. 'Look, Donajski has obviously gone somewhere else. We're taking off. Let me call someone for you, you probably shouldn't drive.'

He pauses, my breathing is more regular.

'Anita,' I say. He clicks his pen. '623-4180'.

He scribbles in his notepad. 'I'll tell her to hurry. Deep breaths now. Walk around if you can.'

I watch him drive away, a nice man after all. Ron was right; sometimes you really can't tell—and sometimes it's the nicer side that's hidden.

The snow billows through the open door. I hold up my arm and see a tiny, individual flake silhouetted against the dark fabric. Another lands on top, and another, gradually forming a layer on my coat, on the floor and on the upholstery. I breathe slowly, evenly. I step out into the falling snow and lean against the car. The bungalow is completely dark now, the street still and white. Consciousness comes in small waves. Moving boxes. Laughing with Anita. Galleys of type. Fresh ink. A perfect omelette. Ron. I struggle to picture his face and know my answer.

THE NORMAL
BLUR OF MYOPIA

Soft flakes of snow chase each other through the air. Some dangle tenu-
ously from branches, cling to dead, dry leaves, then drift to the icy
ground, adding to the sparse snow cover. But still, snow, finally. Three
days' rain has eaten away the snowbanks, left the laneway slick and
treacherous.

I shuffle across the icy yard, down the slope toward the snowmobile
trail our neighbour makes when he sets his trapline. I walk on the side of
the path where the snow is still crunchy, the tread more firm. Maybe I
should go to work early, but it's Wednesday, my half day off for covering
Monday night town council for *The Post*. There are few enough perks as a
small-town reporter. Besides, I don't want to go into work when I'm so
upset.

My foot slips forward on a patch of ice. My skis and poles clatter to
the ground, but I catch my balance just in time. I should wait until more
snow has fallen before going for a cross-country ski. I should wait until
the ice is covered. I should wait, but I have to get out of the house, away
from him. Charles. And there's nowhere else to go.

'Stubborn,' I mutter to the dormant oak tree. 'He can't stand being
the bad guy.'

Yesterday, his daughter Bonnie and her friend were caught stealing
lunch money out of another kid's desk. Her grade-three teacher phoned
me and we agreed it was out of character, an isolated incident. She gave
Bonnie a week of after-school detentions. I didn't say anything to Bonnie
when she came home. She's his daughter after all, and it's tough enough

being the stepmother. It's tough enough being a friend-aunt-babysitter, not being the real mother but doing the real work. When I met Charles, Bonnie was part of the package and I loved them both. I thought I could be helpful, useful. I thought they needed me.

Last night, I asked Charles to speak to Bonnie but he refused. He said she'd already been punished at school. I let it go, too tired to argue, but this morning it irked: she's his daughter after all.

'Just have a quiet word with her,' I said. 'I think it will mean more if you tell her it was wrong.'

'There's no need to tell her twice. She knows now.'

'But she needs to hear it from you, Charles. She needs to know you support the school's decision.'

'Are we out of chili sauce?' he asked, piercing his egg yolk with a fork.

Typical. If it's unpleasant, he ignores it.

I walk toward the Ski-Doo trail.

It's the little things that wear you down: the constant bickering, the litany of arguments, always the same half-dozen subjects. I keep a list at the back of my address book in the empty X, Y and Z pages: parenting (his inability to provide discipline), chores (his unwillingness to do any), sex (my refusal), going out (his refusal). Each time we have a round I put a check mark under the appropriate category. Parenting is a distant second. Sex (my refusal) is winning hands down these days (✓ ✓ ✓ ✓).

Once Charles clipped out articles about sex—how many times a week most couples have it (2.1)—and left it on my dresser. We never talk about it.

The battle of the sexes fought between the sheets. Two-point-one indeed. They may start out there, but then ... we all know the reality.

Last week, I read a survey in one of Anita's trashy mags asking women why they refused to have sex with their partner. The most prevalent answer (58%) was too tired. Number two (21%) was boredom. Third (8%) was their partner's lack of expertise. Then there were a bunch of other reasons: fear of pregnancy, being overweight, anxious they might wake the children, et cetera. I would be hard pressed to pick any one reason. Maybe all of the above. Plus the squabbling, the endless domestic disputes. How can you make love when you've been crabbing at each other all day? And then there's the constant availability. It's comforting to sleep with Charles, to know he is there beside me in the dark. But I hate being at his sexual beck and call, the wham-bam-thank-you-ma'am humiliation of it. I want intimacy, passion. Mutual passion.

Maybe I expect too much. Maybe this domestic purgatory is inevitable in marriage, part of the package to be endured along with the positive: security, someone to share a life with, to love. Family.

I slip my boots into the bindings of my cross-country skis and close them. It's so beautiful out here; the valley circles me like I'm in the centre of a white china bowl. The sun blinks through the clouds illuminating the iced trail, a satin ribbon winding its way down the valley. I step into the tracks I made last weekend—now frozen solid—and sort my poles, hand through the loop, over the top. My right ski suddenly slides forward; I can't stop it. Metal pole tips rattle against ice, one foot slips, then the other and I'm falling, falling. I fall … ice … bum … back … head. Rock-hard ice.

I lie still on the frozen snow, wheezing, struggling to regain my breath. Pain stabs under my ribs, through my lungs. My breath comes in short, white puffs. I concentrate on breathing. In. Pause. Out. Snow melts on my warm cheeks, smudges my glasses. I breathe—in, pause, out—until the pain subsides. The back of my head feels tender, bruised. I turn away from the snowflakes and blink at the stalks of dead grass sticking out of the ice.

The grass is flickering, like a television with poor reception.

I shut my eyes tight, reopen. It's the same. I take my glasses off. Light flashes at the edge of my left eye. Oh God. I close that eye, peer out of my right. The light is gone. Just the normal blur of myopia. I close my right; the flickering, the flashing continues.

Charles drives too fast down the slick back roads to our optometrist in Madawan. He's a good driver, knows how to pull out of the icy spins. He finds a parking spot in front of Schwab's office.

'It's probably nothing,' I say. I don't want any fuss. 'You go ahead to work. I'll walk down to the paper after.'

'Are you sure?' he asks. 'Don't be a martyr, Wanda.'

I smile. He knows me so well in some ways.

'Yeah.' I kiss his cheek. 'I'll call if I need you.'

Schwab says I have to see a retina specialist in the city. He says he doesn't have the equipment or expertise to really figure out what's wrong. His receptionist haggles on the phone until she gets me an appointment for the next morning. So soon. But Schwab didn't seem too concerned.

———————

'There's no use worrying, honey,' Charles says as I get into bed. 'It's probably nothing and you'll know for sure tomorrow.'

He rolls over and falls asleep. I lie in the dark, my mind drifting to a day in seventh grade in Edmonton when my teacher, Mr Campbell, made us pretend we were disabled—'handicapped' we called it in those days. The idea was to penetrate our adolescent self-absorption and instill some empathy, some appreciation of the obstacles faced by others. Some of my classmates stuffed cotton in their ears; others swung through the halls on crutches. I had to be blind for a whole day—the worst assignment. I always get the short stick. Bad Luck Wanda Stewart, that's me. Mr Campbell took my glasses, put cotton pads over my eyes, and tied a scarf around my head. I remember the smell of him, his chest pressed against my back and arm, warm and heavy. 'No peeking until final bell,' he whispered in my ear. He gave me a retractable white stick, his hand brushing mine, emitting sparks. Then he was gone.

I fall into a dream. It's lunch, and Janet, who is playing at being deaf—though of course she can hear fine with only some cotton balls stuffed in her ears—guides me out of the school toward home. I'm crossing 118th Avenue, one of those impossibly wide prairie streets that you have to sprint across to make the light. Suddenly, in the dream, Janet is gone. Cars honk. Someone yells, 'Ya idiot! Get off the road!' I put my hands out in front of me, looking for something solid to cling to and feel a car's breeze as it passes by, a long horn ...

I wake, blink open my eyes and stare at the familiar dark shapes in the bedroom. Dresser, Chair. Bureau. I hear Charles's regular breathing and my heart pounding.

———

My appointment is at ten but I know it's going to be a long wait. The place is packed with grey-haired men and women, squinting under the fluorescent lights. I'm thirty-three, too young to be here. A busty technician sporting a 1970s Farrah Fawcett hairdo puts two sets of stinging drops in my eyes. My pupils dilate. I can't focus, can't read. I put on my prescription Ray-Bans and sit there, watching everyone else in the room, listening to their conversations about gall bladders and gout. I wonder where you could possibly get a Farrah Fawcett haircut these days. Is there a salon that specializes in vintage cuts? David Bowie mullet? Dolly Parton bouffant? Audrey Hepburn pixie?

Finally the receptionist calls me. Dr MacDonald is young, high-school-young, with red hair and freckles. Way too young to be a doctor, much less a specialist. He leans me way back in the chair and peers into my eye with a blinding light. I try not to blink, not to think. Then he gets out a piece of round glass and leans in for a closer look. His breath is warm, smells of mints.

He pulls the chair upright, busies himself putting the glass in a velvet case, says I have lattice degeneration in my left eye. The edges of the retina are starting to deteriorate. It's common in people with myopia, he says.

'And it's causing the flashes?' I ask.

'Maybe,' he says. 'You may also have presumed ocular histoplasmosis in both eyes.'

Says it as if I have split ends.

'How do you spell that?' I ask, ever the reporter.

He writes it down on a piece of pink paper. 'It's caused by a fungus,' he says, 'carried in old, buried poultry excrement.'

'Really?' I say. 'Chicken shit?'

Dr MacDonald explains that the virus scars the retina. Later the scars weaken; a blow can break them open. That's why I see the shining light—holes in my left eye.

He says he's going to close the holes with a laser beam before they get bigger. We'll do it tomorrow, he says. More may develop, he adds. He tells me not to worry, lots of people have it and they see just fine. He pats my arm. I feel cold.

On the drive home, all I can think about is what it would be like to be blind. I'm crying before I cross the bridge over the hydro flood bay.

————————

Charles is working late at the factory; he has to talk with workers on the evening shift about a new line. Then he has gentlemen's hockey. I keep hoping he'll phone, though I know he won't. I'm asleep by the time he gets in. The next morning I tell him what the doctor said. He says he'll try to help more with Bonnie. I've heard that before—I've heard almost everything in three years of marriage—but I hug him anyway. He is trying.

I ask if he'll take the day off to drive me to the clinic for the laser treatment. Dr MacDonald said I shouldn't have any trouble driving home but I'm skeptical. Charles says he has to prepare for a teleconference with the CEO.

'Ask Anita,' he says.

I almost say the meeting isn't until Monday, and surely this is more important, but I don't say anything. I don't have the strength to argue with him. He asks how I'm feeling, but midway through my third sentence he starts turning pages in *Manufacturing News*. I tell him he'd better get going to work.

Anita is happy to give me a lift, to help out. She has to buy a new camera lens for the newspaper anyway; she's been putting it off for weeks.

'It's just so terrible,' Anita says. 'So unfair. Listen, if there's anything I can do, you know, even if you just want to talk ...'

I smile vaguely. I cannot talk about it, even to Anita, who has revealed that her husband bores her in bed, that she can't have orgasms with him anymore. I can tell Anita and Charles what's going on, but I can't talk about my fears. It might make them too real, too clear. Like when I put on my glasses and everything far away suddenly comes into focus, becomes part of my world. It's better to keep this vague, blurred.

Anita drops me off and I sit alone in the waiting room. All the same people seem to be there again. Waiting. Wondering about their future, their vision. The lady puts in my drops. I can't read, can't see really. All I can do is worry. What will happen? Will it hurt? Finally I'm called into the laser room. A coffin-shaped machine takes up most of the space. Dr MacDonald points to a chair in front of it and shows me where to rest my chin and forehead. It looks like an instrument of torture with all those straps, something out of *A Clockwork Orange*.

'I'm not ready for this,' I whisper, my voice breaking.

He hands me a Kleenex. It's then that I realize I am crying.

'Is your husband here?' he asks.

'No, I'm all alone.'

He explains the procedure; his low voice is deliberately slow as if he's speaking to a hysterical child. He's not too far off. He says I could have had a retinal detachment, that I'm lucky we found the holes so quickly. I don't feel lucky, but after a while I feel calmer. After all, what choice do I have? He tells me to sit perfectly still. He sits opposite me, on the other side of the machine, peering through a lens.

Retinal detachment.

I hear loud clicks and see the most amazing lights, purple-pink, magenta—vibrant, almost tactile colour. For a second my eye feels hot, then it is over. He tells me to make an appointment for the next week so he can see how it's healing.

———

I try to stay calm with Charles but I find myself getting angry again and again. He dipped into our savings for hockey fees. (Money ✓) Not that it really matters; he could replace it next pay—if I told him to. That's what peeves me. I'd have to tell him to do it. I run the house, always assumed I would because he seemed so overwhelmed with work and looking after Bonnie. I remember joking with Anita that Charles was living-impaired. Except it wasn't really a joke. I accepted this when we married, but over the years he's grown even less capable. He balks at the simplest tasks, refuses to take responsibility.

I ask Charles to help me sweep the basement. (Chores ✓)

'It's a waste of time,' he says. 'It will just get dirty again when I put in the next load of wood. Wait till spring.'

'But it's filthy,' I say. 'The dirt gets tracked through the whole house and then I have to clean it.'

He shrugs and opens his *Ottawa Star*.

'Are you just lazy?' I ask, vying for a reaction.

He glares over the top of his paper. 'Are you a ball-breaker?'

'What?'

He drops the newspaper to his lap, stares at me over his glasses. 'Is this what I have to do for sex?' he asks in a low monotone.

'What the hell does it have to do with sex?' I reply.

The newspaper rustles in reply. He's stopped talking. (Sex ✓) Now he'll give me the silent treatment. He'll talk to me about what we're having for supper, or whose turn it is to take the dog to the vet. The necessities, that's all. I shouldn't have pushed him.

Last fall we didn't speak for nearly two months. By the time we made up I'd forgotten what we were fighting about. Understanding him is like trying to read a closed book.

I don't remember exactly when these fights began. Don't remember when I started keeping the checklist, trying to be objective and practical. I recall frozen moments, never thawed, never resolved.

Spring days. The yard a muddy swamp. 'Please take off your boots,' I plead. 'It

— 169 —

makes such a mess on the floor.' I'd wet a rag and wipe the muddy boot prints tracked across the kitchen floor, up the stairs to his den. And it would happen again and again and again. Wearing me down so I'd shriek at him, 'Take off your boots for god's sake!' (Chores ✓) Hating myself for sounding like Dad.

Charles, growling at me in the late night, 'You should have told me you were sexually burned out before we got married.' (Sex ✓)

In from grocery shopping on a rainy spring day; water dripping onto the floor, damp paper bags ripping. 'Hello,' I call out. 'Can I get some help?' Muffled sounds come from the TV room. Grocery bags spill over the kitchen table. I return to the car, sleet freezing on my glasses. Again and again I trudge out to get the week's groceries which I have bought and will now unpack and put away, which I will then prepare into nourishing dinners for them, the two of them, Charles and Bonnie, sitting there watching a rerun of Star Trek. *(Chores ✓ Parenting ✓ Common decency!)*

These moments accumulate exponentially.

———

My eyes seem fine these days—no flashes or anything. They're a bit tired sometimes, especially if I read too much, but I read anyway, more than ever. I plough through two or three books a week. That way I don't have to talk to Charles. And you never know … I try not to think about the histoplasmosis, but it's always there, growing in my mind. I call the city CNIB and ask about services in Madawan. There aren't any.

When I'm not reading, I spend most of my time in the workshop, fooling around with my woodwork, my hobby, making wooden coffee tables. 'Sensuous tables' I call them. The legs are twisted, forked branches, useless for anything but firewood. The tops are beautifully grained cross-sections from large trees. I've sold a few at specialty furniture shops in Toronto. Charles's dad taught me about woodworking and when he died two years ago, he left all his tools to me. I love my workshop: the shelves and neat stacks of tools. The solitude.

I finish sanding a table and check the cupboard for varnish—I use a special kind, all-natural, made from Chinese nuts. I reach for some on the top shelf and a plastic bag filled with old brushes falls on my head. I sit on the workbench. I have to be careful. My eyes could develop more holes.

After supper I lie on our bed reading Sherlock Holmes stories. I piece the details together, figuring out which ones are important. Midway through 'The Speckled Band' I notice a black spot on the page. I close my left eye; the spot is gone. I close my right eye; it's back again. It doesn't move—it's not a speck of dirt. I focus on the sheets, the white wall. The black spot. I dial the after-hours number Dr MacDonald gave me and his answering service says he'll call me back.

Back in the bedroom, I open the window a crack. A frigid draft pierces the stale room, cooling my face and bare forearms. Goosebumps rise to meet the cold. It's so damned unfair. Why me? Children play in the dirt—Christ, they do it every day. I didn't take any chances. I have bad luck. First with Dad, then men in general. Now this. Life isn't fair. That's what Anita says. She's right, of course. She says it's a matter of making the most of what life delivers. Of being smart about what you want.

Dr MacDonald calls. He says he'll see me in the clinic at eight the next morning. He says not to worry. He might as well tell me not to breathe.

I wait up for Charles, mostly because I'm too anxious to sleep. I tell him I have a black spot. Another one. I try not to cry.

'I have an appointment at eight tomorrow,' I say.

'Who's going to look after Bonnie?' he asks. 'It's a PD day—no school.'

I stare at him. What is he thinking? That I should stay home? That I should make arrangements? That this, too, is my responsibility?

I lie down in bed, pulling the duvet around my shoulders. Anita would say I haven't been smart about getting what I want.

'I *guess* I can take the morning off,' Charles says finally.

He's incapable of handling anything this traumatic, this serious. It's who he is. He's lingering still in those first two decades of life.

Emotionally, he can't move past the self-absorption of youth, the feeling that the world owes him an easy, uncomplicated life with maximum control and minimal responsibility. Then his mother and her illness let him down. Joy let him down by walking out. His father died. And now I'm making demands on him.

I try to understand, but then he climbs into bed without his pyjama bottoms. I turn my back to him and fume in the darkness. (Sex ✓)

———

In the car I spill coffee all over my new Billie Holiday cassette. The clinic is deserted. Dr MacDonald flashes the glass disk in my eye, prods my eyeball with his forefinger so he can see all the edges. I dig my nails into my palm, nearly piercing the flesh.

'There's a new development,' he says.

Like it's a twist in the plot. Another piece of evidence to consider.

He explains that a blood vessel is growing into my fovea. 'Sometimes that happens in areas that are heavily scarred. It's trying to bring blood to the damaged area. We'll have to stop it or it will block your vision.'

'Block?'

'If it keeps growing, you'll lose the central vision.'

He draws a picture for me. A blood vessel, tiny, seeking. Destroying in its attempt to nurture.

He starts up the laser; its dull drone is powerful, serious. I rest my chin in the cup, forehead against the straps. I stare at my twisted reflection in the chromed machine. He writes something on my chart.

'I'm going to cauterize the vessel,' he finally says. 'Then I'm going to build a ridge of scar tissue to protect the fovea. It's very delicate. You have to stay still.'

'Yes,' I say, surprised by the strength in my voice.

The light comes again and again. Magenta at first, then I lose the colour. All I feel are sharp jabs in the dark like a thousand needles, again and again.

'That should do it,' he says at last.

I lean back, blink. My eye feels pierced. I glance down at my faded blue jeans: the black spot is still there. It always will be, but maybe Dr MacDonald has stopped it from growing.

'Thank you,' I say.

He nods. 'Now keep a lookout for new black spots. The vessel could start growing again. You never know.'

My throat closes in; I cannot speak.

Bonnie watches TV downstairs while I rest in bed with a damp, musty-smelling washcloth over my eyes. I lie there, trying not to think or dream. When I open my eyes it's dark outside. The alarm clock glows 5:42. I go downstairs and begin peeling potatoes. For once, Charles comes home promptly at six. He doesn't ask how it went at the clinic and I don't say anything. Bonnie comes in and starts chattering about her TV program. I'm distracted and burn the pork tenderloin. Charles gives me one of his looks as I scrape off the char. I stare back coldly. Pin-point pupils.

Supper is a mournful affair. Bonnie pushes the food around her plate. Who could blame her? The meat is burned, the potatoes overdone and mealy, the winter green beans tasteless. Bonnie asks to be excused and runs upstairs. I scrape my own dinner into the dog's bowl. I feel sick. Where did it all go wrong?

Charles sits, watching me.

'Are you really that miserable?' he asks.

'I don't understand what you expect,' I reply. 'You obviously don't want to be part of my life. I mean, you aren't even interested in what happened today at the clinic. I don't think you care.'

'Of course I care,' he says.

'Yeah, you care about how it will affect you.' I pause for a moment and look at my husband. 'What do you expect from me anyway?'

'What do you mean?'

'I mean, what's your idea of the perfect wife?'

Why didn't I ask him this question years ago, before we married? But then I was in the throes of limerence and on the rebound from Ron. I was sure Charles was the one.

He pauses for a moment, squashing his mashed potatoes with his fork.

'I guess she'd be self-sufficient and sexually willing. Those are the two main things.'

'Self-sufficient! You mean like a roommate? But also willing to have sex on demand. And is that all?'

'Those are just the main things; there are other things too. You know, a good mother and all that.'

I grind my teeth.

'Now don't get all excited,' he says. 'You're just upset because of your appointment. Why don't you tell me what happened?'

My face is hot, flushed. My voice quavers. 'You want me to be self-sufficient? I'll do it. I'll handle this myself, but it works both ways. You better learn to be self-sufficient, too. You better learn to take care of your own needs.'

'What the hell is that supposed to mean?'

'It means that if you won't give me the emotional support I need, then I won't give you the sex you need. Seems pretty equitable, don't you think?'

'Why don't you just leave if you're so damned unhappy?' he shouts, jabbing his index finger in the air between us.

I refuse to let my tears fall, brush them away roughly, start stacking the dishes.

This is all I need. Shit. Every time things get really rough he asks if I'm going to leave. I guess that's what happens to some people who have been divorced: they lose confidence, always think it'll happen again. How many times has he asked me? Twenty? Thirty? Each time I've been overwhelmed and immediately tried to make things better. But this time I don't feel sad. I'm angry. Fed up. He says it because it's part of the game and my role is to give in, to appease him. I turn to him.

'Is that what you want, Charles? Do you want me to leave?'

He pauses a second. His face doesn't reveal a thing but I know he's surprised.

'All I want is for us to get along,' he says too loudly in the still house.

I begin running water into the sink. All I can think of is leaving my home, leaving Bonnie behind. I've invested so much in this. My energy, my love, my youth.

'Let's not quarrel,' he says. 'You're upset about your eyes.'

He walks over and puts his hands on my shoulders. I shrug him away and begin wiping the table. It's amazing the mess three people can make.

And where does love enter into all of this? I remember how I used to love him. I loved him for the ways he was different from me—his seemingly easygoing nature, his ability to focus on what mattered to him and ignore everything else. But I ended up wanting him to be just like me: organized, practical, efficient. It's like we're all petty household gods, trying to re-create each other in our own image.

Charles isn't talking to me but I don't give a damn. I have nothing to say to him.

The marital house of cards is tumbling: 8 of sex, 10 of chores, 4 of parenting, queen of socializing. Tumbling, tumbling onto the dirty linoleum. It would take too much time and energy to reconstruct. Besides, the cards are too worn and dog-eared to build anything.

I should leave, I know I should, but what about my eyes? What if I lose my sight? I'll need him, someone, to help me, won't I? But not Charles. No.

———

Not only is it busy at *The Post* with Anita away on holiday, I also have a dozen or so backorders for tables. I'm busier than at Christmas. I cook dinner, eat, then go to my shop to finish sanding and varnishing. My tables are getting bigger, more elaborate, and I've started experimenting with paint. I mix that magenta, the one I see when Dr MacDonald lasers my eyes. I paint jagged holes and squiggles on a black background. I try different colours, textures, working late into the night, loving it, listening to the radio or old jazz tapes—Sarah Vaughan, Dinah Washington—and avoiding Charles. I tiptoe to bed, carefully stepping around the squeaky floorboard near the door. He's always asleep.

My eyes seem to be doing fine. I don't even see the black spot. It's remarkable how my right eye has completely compensated for the spot of lost vision in my left. My next appointment isn't for six months.

———

On Charles's hockey night, I quit working early and go to bed to read for an hour or two. I open the window in the bedroom, brushing aside the dead cluster flies. There's a real smell of spring in the air: decaying leaves, dampness, melting dog shit. A breeze floats through the stale room, touches my face and bare forearms. I sit down on the edge of the bed, my face toward the window. I look out at the half moon and it's marred by a black spot. A new one? I close my right eye. There are two spots now, the old one small in comparison. I begin to weep uncontrollably, gasping for breath like a small child.

Dr MacDonald says to meet him at the clinic at eight again. I lie in bed, staring at the ceiling. Charles slips into bed after twelve, stinking of beer. I pretend to be asleep, concentrate on breathing regularly. I'm in this alone. Finally, I doze for a few hours before dawn. I don't dream. I wake up before his alarm goes off and slip out of the house quietly without leaving a note.

At the clinic, I wait for the drops to dilate my pupils, clutching the edges of my chair. Dr MacDonald says it's the same thing, another blood vessel growing into the fovea. He says this time it's even closer and my stomach lurches. He lasers again, but this time he's not so optimistic.

'I may not have stopped it. I was afraid to go too close. Keep an eye on it.'

An eye. Which eye? *Keep an eye out. See you later.* Sight platitudes race through my mind.

I sit in the waiting room for a while, looking out the window over the patches of snow clinging to the roof vents and elevator shaft. I wait for the drops to wear off. I wait for the vessel to grow. I know I will lose the sight in that eye. My nose tickles, lips purse. Tears sting the winter-dried skin on my cheeks.

But I still have the other eye, the better one really, the stronger one. I still have that.

Acknowledgements

The following stories were previously published, in slightly different form:

'Best Before' (*Shift*, 1993)

'Dispatches' (*The New Quarterly*, 1995)

'Fresh Hell of Christmas' (part of *Kitchen Chronicles*, an online novel in 52 instalments published at *Ottawa Magazine*, December 2013)

'Funeral Hats' (*Zygote*, Summer 1999)

'Comet, It Tastes Like Gasoline' (*The Antigonish Review*, Summer 2001)

'Peeling the Artichoke' (*The Company We Keep*, Bushek Books, 2004)

'Do You Think She Knows?' (formerly 'Waiting', *Ottawa Magazine*, Summer 2015)

'The Normal Blur of Myopia' (formerly 'Seeing', *The Capilano Review*, Spring 1995)

Parts of 'Comet, It Tastes Like Gasoline' and 'Up in the Air, Junior Birdmen' appear in the author's novel *Regarding Wanda* (2006)

The lyrics cited in 'Peeling the Artichoke' are from 'Hard Times Come Again No More', written by Stephen Foster and published in 1855.

Thanks

For their thoughtful critiquing and advice, I am grateful to my generous writer friends including Diane Schoemperlen, Mark Frutkin, Roger Collier, Kathlyn Bradshaw, Debra Martens, and the Ottawa Writing Group. A special thanks to the Ontario Arts Council for its financial and moral support. I am also indebted to my meticulous editor, Stephanie Small, and the talented people at the Porcupine's Quill. And finally, thanks to my husband, Stuart Kinmond, for his tireless support and encouragement.

About the Author

Barbara Sibbald is a Canadian novelist and an award-winning journalist. She has published two works of fiction, *The Book of Love: Guidance in Affairs of the Heart* (General Store Publishing House) and *Regarding Wanda* (Bunkhouse Press). The latter was short-listed for the Ottawa Book Award.

Sibbald has published numerous short stories in anthologies and literary journals such as *Shift, The Capilano Review, The Antigonish Review* and *The New Quarterly.* Two of her short stories have been nominated for the Journey Prize in fiction writing.

She is, perhaps, more widely known for her non-fiction journalism, including her extensive writing on health, medical and lifestyle issues, published widely in the *Canadian Medical Association Journal,* where she also works as an editor. She has also been a regular contributor to the *Ottawa Citizen* and the *The Huffington Post,* and is a contributor to other major Canadian media outlets, such as the *The Globe and Mail* and *Ottawa Magazine.*

Barbara Sibbald has twice been cited for the Michener Award for meritorious public service in journalism; has been recognized with the Canadian Association of Journalists' investigative journalism prize (2006); and has twice won gold awards for breaking news from the Canadian Business Press.

She lives in Ottawa with her husband, the artist Stuart Kinmond.